Clarence W Hobbs

Lynn and the Surroundings

Clarence W Hobbs

Lynn and the Surroundings

ISBN/EAN: 9783337191764

Printed in Europe, USA, Canada, Australia, Japan

Cover: Foto ©Andreas Hilbeck / pixelio.de

More available books at **www.hansebooks.com**

LYNN

AND

SURROUNDINGS

BY

Clarence W. Hobbs.

———

ILLUSTRATED.

———

- -1886. —

PUBLISHERS
228
LEWIS & WINSHIP
UNION ST.
LYNN MASS.

Index.

List of Illustrations.

LYNN and SURROUNDINGS,

High Rock.

OVERLOOKING the town of Lynn,
So far above that the city's din
Mingles and blends with the heavy roar
Of the breakers along the curving shore;
Scarred and furrowed and glacier-seamed
Back in the ages so long ago
The boldest philosopher never dreamed
To count the centuries' ebb and flow;
Stands a rock, with its gray old face
Eastward ever turned, to the place
Where first the rim of the sun is seen,
Whenever the morning sky is bright,
Cleaving the glistening, glancing sheen
Of the sea with a disc of insufferable light.
Down in the earth its roots strike deep;
Up to his breast the houses creep,
Climbing e'en to his rugged face,
Or nestling lovingly at his base.

Stand on his forehead, bare and brown;
Send your gaze o'er the roofs of the town
Away to the line, so faint and dim,
Where the sky stoops down to the crystal rim
Of the broad Atlantic, whose billows toss,
Wrestling and weltering and hurrying on
With awful fury, whenever across
His broad, bright surface, with howl and moan,
The tempest whirls, with black wing bowed
To the yielding waters which fly to the cloud,
Or hurry along, with thunderous shocks,
To break on the ragged and riven rocks.

When the tide comes in on a sunny day,
You can see the waves break back in spray
From the splintered spurs of Phillips' Head;
Or, tripping along with dainty tread,
As of a million glancing feet,
Shake out the light in a quick retreat;
Or along the smooth curve of the beach,
Snowy and curling, in long lines reach
An islet, anchored and held to land
By a glistening, foam-fringed ribbon of sand —
That is Nahant, and that hoary ledge
To the left is Egg Rock, like a blunted wedge
Cleaving the restless ocean's breast,
And bearing the light-house on its crest.

— ELIZABETH L. MERRILL.

LYNN AND SURROUNDINGS

L YNN is like no other New England city. Both in situation and surroundings, she has a beauty and a charm all her own, and in her natural physical characteristics is displayed a marked individuality. All the varied scenes of town, sea-shore and country are found within her borders. "The farmer drives his team afield" not far from the stirring mart, and the fisherman mends his nets in sight of the towering, smoke-wreathed chimneys of the large factories. But a short distance northward from the City Hall are bosky dells between the hills where one may hide, and many peaceful lakes where the wanderer may catch the reflection of wooded shore and shadowy cloud; while nearer still, in the opposite direction, is the smooth beach, where one may walk the shining sand, plunge beneath the curling breakers, or from the neighboring cliff count the sails and watch the mighty pulsations of the restless heart of ocean, as with ceaseless throbs she sends the wavelets hurrying toward the shore. Or, better still, if one has but an hour for sight-seeing, let him climb the stairs to the top of the rugged observatory built by nature, ages before man built the town, and a wondrous panorama unfolds before his eyes. At his feet lie the city and the shore; on the landward side the view is limited only by the dark background of evergreen-clad hills, while toward the sea the scene dies away in the purple haze which hangs like a veil over the bosom of the ocean. No point of view on the Atlantic gives a larger return for so little effort, and no other city of the New World can boast of such an endless variety of landscape and sea-view, hill and valley, lake and river, cottage-crowned cliff and rock-bound shore, with the bright waters of the bay dimpling and sparkling in the sunlight. On a clear day the scene is full of life and light, and is inspiring and exhilarating in a high degree. But when the storm cloud hangs over the waters, and the huge waves seem to gather their forces for a final assault upon the opposing rocks, and the spray flies in clouds far up on the shore, the scene is full of grandeur.

Let us together visit High Rock, and see these things for ourselves. One hundred and seventy feet to the top; and approached from the northward, the ascent is gradual and easy; but on the seaward side both wind and limb get well tested, though the climb is now facilitated by successive flights of steps set in an iron frame-work upon the face of the cliff.

There was once a wooden tower on the summit of the rock, but one night it disappeared in smoke; and now we take our stand upon the bare rock, or lean against the flag-staff. The eye naturally turns first toward the sea. At the left is the village of Swampscott, with its cluster of fishing-boats and white beach covered with dories and fishing-nets spread out to dry. Further out is Baker's Island, with its light, the white towers of Marblehead, and on a clear day is seen the distant headland of Cape Ann. Off to the right are the dark brown monument of Bunker Hill and the gilded dome on Beacon Hill. Further to the north we get a glimpse of Wachusett rising above the succession of lesser hills, and to the south the Blue Hills of Milton lie misty in the distance. Nearer stretches out the graceful curve of Crescent Beach, and directly in front of us

MAPLE STREET, GLENMERE.

is the harbor, its bounds determined on the one hand by the Point of Pines, and on the other by the dark rocks of the Nahants — those twin gems of the North Shore, connected with the mainland only by a narrow neck of sand —

"A snowy ribbon, fringed with foam."

Lying low in the waters of the bay, seemingly no larger than a fisherman's dory, is Egg Rock, with its white light-house, for thirty years a faithful sentinel on a dangerous coast. Around to the northeast are seen the hills and plains of

Danvers and Peabody, while through a gap in the hills we catch a glimpse of our near neighbor, Salem. Back from the town stretch a ledgy range of hills — of which High Rock is the most easterly — their sides clothed with dark green trees, save where these have given way to beautiful cottages, and occasionally a more stately residence; and each of them has its name: Lover's Leap, a steep cliff one hundred feet high from its base, and one hundred and thirty from the sea level; Pine Hill, two hundred and twenty-four feet high, at the southwestern extremity of which is Saddler's Rock, one hundred and sixty feet high; and among them are the Pirates' Cave, Dungeon Rock, Glen Lewis, and many other beautiful spots made doubly interesting by the halo of legend and romance which surrounds their names.

At our feet lies the city, circling around on either side and climbing the sides of the hill until many of its houses nestle under the very edge of the rock on which we stand. Northeast of us lie the pretty villages of Wyoma and Glenmere, and the once beautiful lake, bearing the musical name of the Indian maiden, Wenuchus. In its waters our foremothers rotted their flax, whence came its more practical and homely name. Now the useful but prosaic ice-house sadly mars the symmetry of its shores. Further to the east Gold-fish

GOLD-FISH POND, FAYETTE STREET.

Pond lies like a gem in the sunlight, while crowning the eminence which overlooks the bay are hundreds of beautiful residences, half hid among the leafy branches of the elms and maples. Directly to the southwest, between us and the harbor, is the manufacturing district. At this distance we hear little of the noise of the city, but we can see the busy life as it pours up and down the streets. The buildings have a substantial and prosperous appearance, and are admirably adapted to the great industry of the city. What a contrast between these solid structures of brick and the low wooden shops in which the shoe business of Lynn was transacted before the trade of shoemaking had been evolved into a science! As we turn toward the west, we see that the circus-field of our boyhood has become thickly populous; and over the thick-leaved trees of the Common, which, from this standpoint, hide the shape thereof —so appropriate to the City of Shoes—we can see the white-walled homes of West Lynn stretching far out toward the Saugus River; and beyond, as the sun is setting, we catch a glimpse of the shadowy hills and salty flats of the towns beyond. In our sweep we have counted the spires of the churches and the towers of the school-houses, admired the proportions of the City Hall, and marked where the two roads stretch their converging lines of rails toward Boston. We can dimly see the gray stones in the old Burying Ground, where sleep the worthies of the colonial days, and to the north, gleaming fair, the white monuments of the more modern but equally silent city of the dead.

There is little in this busy modern city to remind us that it has a history, and that the white man first trod the spot where we stand, more than two centuries and a half ago. The city of the fathers is no more—gone out as com-pletely and permanently as the ways and methods of the cordwainers who first plied their trade in her little shops. The makers of the labor-saving machines made over the somewhat scattered and straggling town of Lynn into a thriving and prosperous city, which refuses to believe the census-taker who says we have not yet fifty thousand inhabitants.

FOOT OF NAHANT STREET.

Saugus.

WHAT time the first white man set his foot upon the soil of Lynn, or who he was, history revealeth not. Legends of a visit by Thorwald, with a company of sturdy Norsemen, to Nahant in the eleventh century, as well as tales of explorations in these waters by the early English adventurers, Gosnold and Pring, are preserved; but their foundation is obscure, if not doubtful. It is reasonably certain, however, that in 1614 Capt. John Smith, having established his Virginia colony, sailed northward on a voyage of exploration; and in his excellent description of the coast, he mentions the Mattahunts as two islands of great beauty, and gives such a minute description of the bay and surroundings as to leave little doubt that he explored the beautiful peninsula, but had mistaken the pronunciation of the Indian name, Nahanteau. In 1622 the whole territory known as the Massachusetts, extending ten miles northeast from the Charles River, including Saugus and the Nahants, was granted to Capt. Robert Gorges; but he failed to perfect his title to his princely domain, and left his heirs only a series of vexatious lawsuits, which were decided against them. The settlement of Salem was begun in 1625 by the famous Roger Conant, who came thither with the remnant of the Cape Ann colony. On the 19th of March, 1628, the Council in England sold all that part of Massachusetts

CLIFF ROCK, NEAR PEABODY LINE.

between three miles north of the Charles River and three miles south of the Merrimack to a company of six gentlemen, among whom was Mr. John Humphrey, who afterward became an honored citizen of Lynn. Until that time the Indians had held undisputed possession of the country. Essex County was included in

the domain of Nanapashemet, the mighty chief of the Pawtuckets, who sometimes made his home near the falls of the Merrimack, and occasionally on Sagamore Hill, at the eastern end of our city. But in a long and bloody war with the Tarratines, those terrible fighters of eastern New England, Nanapashemet, the New Moon, had gone down in a crimson sky ; and a terrible scourge, occurring shortly after, had so reduced the numbers of the Indians that when the first settlers came, there were only scattering villages here and there, presided over by local sachems, and the old warlike spirit of the noble red men had given place to a more peaceful disposition, and a readiness to receive whatever in the way of benefits the hand of the white men might bring. They were entirely willing to sell whatever land the settlers desired, and did not hesitate to sell the same parcel as many times over as they could find a purchaser — a practice prolific of trouble for the settlers and business for the courts. The Indians are represented to have been tall and well-formed, and one impressionable writer speaks of "the unparalleled beauty" of the Indian maidens, describing them as having "very good features, seldom without a come-to-me in their countenance, all of them black-eyed, having even, short teeth, and very white, their hair black, thick and long, broad-breasted, handsome, straight bodies, and slender, thin limbs, cleanly, straight, generally plump as a partridge, and, saving now and then one, of modest deportment;" and another says: "The Indesses that are young are some of them very comely. Many prettie Brownettos and spider-fingered lassies may be seen among them." No doubt the national costume of the Indians afforded abundant facilities for accurate personal description.

THE FIRST MAP OF SAUGUS

Lewis, writing in 1844, gravely informs us that Lynn "is much smaller than it was before the towns of Saugus, Lynnfield, Reading and South Reading were separated from it." Since that time the towns of Swampscott and Nahant have taken up separate existence. All the territory comprising these towns was called by the Indians, Saugus. Salem was known as Naumkeag, Marblehead as Massabequash, and the territory lying southwest of Saugus had the musical appellation of Winnisimet, but it was included in the territory of Mystic, which afterward became Boston. The marsh now lying partly in Chelsea and partly in Saugus was called Rumney marsh. When the white men came, Winnepoyekin — the Winnepurkit of Whittier's Bride of Pennacook — eldest son of Nanapashemet,

"He whose name the Mohawk trembling heard,"

ruled the territory of Naumkeag, Montowampate was sachem of Saugus, and Poquanam of Nahant — all of them sons of Nanapashemet. The whites gave these three sagamores the less melodious but more pronounceable names of Sagamore James, Sagamore George No-nose and Duke William. It is evident that the "power and regal consequence" attributed to the Saugus chieftains had failed to impress the settlers as anything overwhelming. Most of the Indians hereabouts lived on Sagamore Hill, near the end of Long Beach, at Swamp-

scott, and at Nahant. Saugus signifies great or extended, and was used by the
Indians to designate the long beach which stretched out in front of their official
residence. The river which now goes by that name was called by the Indians,
Abousett. Nahant is a shortening of the Indian term Nahanteau, signifying the
twins, and for many years the settlers adopted the Indian formula, and spoke
of the two islands as the Nahants. When, therefore, in 1629 — probably in
the leafy month of June — Edmund and Francis Ingalls, not liking the atmosphere of the Endicott settlement at Salem, set out to find a place to " set
themselves downe," under the roving permission, given by the bluff and sometimes peppery Governor, to go where it pleased them, came hitherward searching for a suitable location where they might carve themselves out a home, they
found a broken country, thickly covered with the primeval forest, save where,
here and there, the Indians had cleared small patches, where they planted their
pumpkins, beans and corn. Without doubt they climbed High Rock to get the
lay of the land, and as their eyes drank in the beautiful prospect, perhaps they
felt in their hearts, as Thorwald is said to have done when he landed on Nahant :
" Here it is beautiful, and here I would like to fix my dwelling." Edmund
chose " a fayre plaine " beside a sedgy lakelet, on what is now called Fayette
street, and Francis selected a spot nearer the beach in Swampscott, where he
built the first tannery in New England. Newhall, in his Jewels of the Third
Plantation, gives a charming picture of the building of the first log cabin.
There accompanied Edmund Ingalls from Salem, when he was ready to com-
mence his habitation, a goodly company, who lent willing hands to the work.

The corner stone, or, more properly, the
corner log, was laid with earnest exhorta-
tion and lengthy prayer, and tradition has
it that one Zachariah Hart worked harder,
prayed longer and swore louder than any
other man in the company. Three other
families came to Lynn that year—William
Dixey, who remained here some years,
but finally removed to Salem ; William
Wood, who subsequently left to begin
with others the settlement of Sandwich ;

EARLY HOMES IN SAUGUS.

and John Wood, who lived on the corner
of Essex and Chestnut streets, and from him that locality has ever since been
called Woodend. The Indians received the settlers kindly, and rendered them
assistance in many ways, and, in return, received many benefits from the hands
of the colonists. The following year saw nearly fifty families added to the
number of settlers, who took up land in various portions of the plantation, and
this year was born Thomas Newhall, the first white child who saw the light in
Lynn. These settlers were principally farmers, who brought with them from
England many of the necessaries and comforts of life, and possessed a large
stock of cattle. The sheep, goats and swine were for many years pastured on
Nahant, the danger from catamounts, bears and wolves being so great that the
constant services of a shepherd were required for their protection. The Saugus
freemen took their seats in the General Court in 1630, an act which constituted

all the incorporation the town ever had. The legislators had mostly come from the walks of private life, and were unskilled in the mysteries of statecraft. Besides, the General Court had its calendar full of business, being called upon to regulate many of the most trifling details of everyday life, to say nothing of exercising a general oversight of the religious opinions of the settlers. As a consequence, many things which were well enough were suffered to stand, by common consent. But the progress of the settlers was measurably rapid. Their habitations, which at the first were roughly built of logs and thatched with straw or sedge, were improved; farming tools became more abundant, and preparation was made for the common defense by the organization of a military company, which had two "great sakers," or iron cannon. The surrounding Indians, seeing the growing power of the settlers, had begun to be uneasy and less friendly; although the local sachems continued to regard the settlers kindly, the sad experiences of the other colonies warned the dwellers in Saugus to be on their guard. No outbreak ever occurred in this vicinity, but twenty-six men from Saugus took part in the King Philip war and participated in the swamp fight, which proved the death-blow to the power of the mighty Sassacus.

During the first few years the religious privileges of the settlers were limited, the nearest minister being at Salem, and to
attend service there the settlers had to traverse a road well-nigh
impassable from stumps and rocks. In 1634 the Rev. Stephen
Bachiler came to Saugus, and the First Church was organized.
The first meeting-house was situated on the corner of
Shepard and Summer streets. It was a log building,
set in a hollow for protection from the winds, and like

LAKE WENUCHUS, OR FLAX POND.

many of the early dwelling-houses, the floor was sunk
several feet below the surface of the ground outside, and
entrance was had only by a descent of several steps. Trouble soon arose between Mr. Bachiler and his flock, and in 1636 he was succeeded by Rev. Samuel Whiting, a most godly man. Under his fostering care the church became united and prosperous, and the foundation was laid so deep and strong that the church continues to this day with no substantial change in form or doctrine, the oldest orthodox Congregational Church in the world. The form and appearance of the town has undergone several transformations; new sects

and new doctrines have arisen, few of which remain; but amid all the clash and tumult of sect and faction, and the changes in the customs and manners of the people, the old First Church has stood, a monument to that sturdy Puritan faith which would sooner face the terrors and hardships of a home in the wilderness than oppression and interference in matters of conscience, and which has been transmitted from father to son for ten generations.

With 1637 ends what may be termed the first period of our history. In the eight years of its existence the colony has so rapidly increased in numbers that an assistant to the minister had been installed, farms cleared and stocked, mills built, and a ferry established over the Saugus River; altogether the colony was contented and prosperous.

A GLIMPSE OF THE MARSHES.

"Saugust is called Lin."

SUCH is the quaint and entire official record of the legislation by which our city came to be called by its new name, the action of the General Court necessary thereto taking place on the 15th of November, 1637. The name was given in compliment to Rev. Samuel Whiting, who had come hither from King's Lynn, in England. The name in its original form, *len*, signifying "spreading waters," was thought to be specially applicable to this spot, with its beautiful bays and its nine forest-girt lakelets scattered here and there.

The name was written by the settlers "somewhat according to the taste and fancy of the speller"— Lin, Linn, Lyn, Lynn and Lynne. The liberties taken with the orthography of the word were no greater than was done with most other words of the language, for it seems as though some of the early writers tried to make their manuscripts as grotesque as possible. Some time was required to familiarize the people with the new name. For several years Saugus and Lynn were interchangeable terms, and sometimes the name of the place was written "Lynn at Saugus." Notwithstanding the change of name, the affairs of the colony ran on in their usual and uneventful course. Population gradually increased, better roads were constructed, bridges built, and schools opened, where the boys became acquainted with the rule of three and the

PHAETON ROCK, NEAR LYNNFIELD ROAD.

schoolmaster's ferule, the heroic method of instruction being then the popular idea. Very little attention was given to the education of females, it being deemed of more importance that they should be skilled in domestic arts.

The Iron Works were established in Saugus in 1643, and for several years continued to be the only, as they were the first, manufacture of the kind in the colonies. They continued an eventful but unprofitable existence for many years, the chief obstacle to their success being the scarcity of money among their customers. The ore used was bog iron, which was quite abundant, and the furnaces turned out a good grade of charcoal iron.

ABIJAH BOARDMAN HOMESTEAD IN SAUGUS.

Three years later Lynn was made a market town, and Tuesdays were given to a general interchange of commodities among the inhabitants, and the Market Street occasionally took on an animated appearance, scarcely rivalling, however, the bustle and brilliancy of a modern Saturday evening. Until the years closely following 1650, the settlers had their religious affairs very much their own way, and doubtless thought they had secured the poet's ideal —

"Freedom to worship God."

The teachings of George Fox, and the bitter persecution accorded him in England, had not been unnoted in the New World, and the people had begun to take sides in the controversy when the first Quakers landed in Boston in 1656. The colonial authorities were quick to imitate their English cousins in their methods of dealing with the

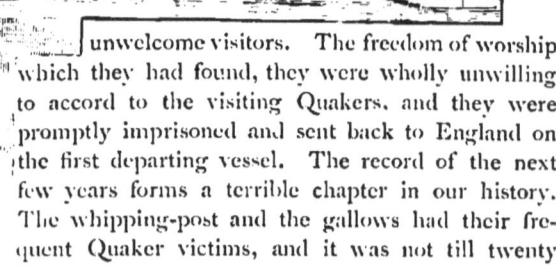

unwelcome visitors. The freedom of worship which they had found, they were wholly unwilling to accord to the visiting Quakers, and they were promptly imprisoned and sent back to England on the first departing vessel. The record of the next few years forms a terrible chapter in our history. The whipping-post and the gallows had their frequent Quaker victims, and it was not till twenty

FLOATING BRIDGE.

years after that the authorities discovered that these were the least effective means ever devised for checking the growth of a religious idea. The Quakers continued to multiply until there were over one hundred families in Lynn, and it was not until opposition was withdrawn and they were left to themselves that they were found to be a simple and harmless body, with many of the ordinary frailties common to our human nature.

Scarcely had the excitement over Quakerism begun to decline when the bugaboo of witchcraft arose to vex the righteous souls of the settlers. Salem village, now a portion of Danvers, was headquarters for the strange delusion, but Lynn was by no means left out in the cold. On the contrary, she took an active part in the strange and terrible tragedies, and furnished her quota of alleged witches, and an occasional wizard. The excitement culminated in 1692, and notwithstanding the violence of the outbreak, subsided as quickly as it had arisen.

GREAT DWARF ROCK, NEAR GLEN LEWIS.

The old log meeting-house, which for half a century served the spiritual needs of the colony, was removed, in 1682, from Shepard street to the center of the Common, and converted into a more pretentious edifice, which, from its peculiar shape, has gone into history by the name of the Old Tunnel. The Rev. Samuel Whiting, for forty years the faithful pastor and earnest preacher, passed to his rest in 1679, and shortly after, the Rev. Jeremiah Shepherd came to fill his post. Mr. Shepherd had few of the characteristics of his predecessor. He was a positive spiritual force, and stirred up the church to greater outward effort and efficacy than it had before shown. But he was also of a fiery and somewhat irascible disposition, and mixed as freely in the worldly as the spiritual contentions of his time. He was a man of strong mental power — a discourse three hours long was not an uncommon feat for him ; but whether this habit was in any way the occasion of the enactment by the General Court of a law compelling everyone to attend meeting, is not stated. But a similar habit on the part of his predecessor was the occasion of this quaint paragraph in the Journal of Obadiah Turner, one of the early lights of Lynn :

"Allen Bridges hath bin chose to wake ye sleepers in meeting, and being much proud of his place, must needs have a fox taile fixed to ye end of a long staff, wherewith he may brush ye faces of them yt will have napps in time of discourse; likewise a sharpe thorne, wherewith he may prick such as be most sounde. On ye laste Lord his day, as hee strutted about ye meeting-house, hee did spy Mr. Tomlins sleeping with much comforte, hys head kept steadie by being in ye corner, and hys hand grasping ye rail. And so spying, Allen did quicklie thrust his staff behind Dame Ballard, and give hjm a grievous prick upon ye hand. Whereupon Mr. Tomlins did spring vpp mch aboue ye floore, and with terrible force strike with hys hand against ye wall, and also, to ye great wonder of all, prophainlie exclaime in a loude voice: 'Cuss ye woodchuck;' he dreaming, as it seemed, yt a woodchuck had seized and bit his hand. But on comeing to know where he was and ye great scandall he had committed, he seemed much abashed, but did not speake. And I think he will not soone againe go to sleepe in meeting. Ye women may sometimes sleepe, and none know it by reason of their enormous bonnets. Mr. Whiting doth pleasantlie say yt from ye pulpit, he doth seeme to be preaching to stacks of straw, with men sitting here and there among them."

In 1683, following the example of their neighbors round about, the people of Lynn succeeded in perfecting their title to their lands, by deed from the heirs of the original Indian proprietors. This deed is recorded at Salem. It is a long and curious document, abounding in surplusage and legal redundancies, on account of which, possibly because few people could unravel their meaning, such documents were thought to be all the more binding. This deed conveyed all the interest which David Kunkshamooshaw and Abigail, his wife, Cicely, better known as Su George, and James Quonopohit—the sole surviving heirs of Nanapashemet—held in the territory of Lynn and Nahant. The signatures of David and Abigail seem to be rude representations of a bow and arrow. The

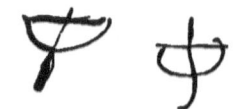      

third signature is that of Cicely. James signed his name in full, after the manner of white men. The last is the sign manual of Mary Ponham, his wife. The settlers attached much importance to the Indian deeds, but Sir Edmund Andros, the English governor, professed the greatest contempt for them, likening them to scratches of a bear's claw, and by an arbitrary exercise of his power, endeavored to set aside the deed of Nahant in favor of his secretary, Edward Randolph, who had coveted the peninsula. The spirit with which his purpose was resisted by the settlers taught him the useful lesson that in this country the government is no stronger than the popular will, and that the ruler who undertakes to breast public opinion, right or wrong, has a wearisome, and possibly a dangerous, course to follow. Randolph persisted in his claim, and finally, finding himself vigorously opposed by Oliver Purchis, lost his temper, and attempted to cut off the ears of his opponent. This was more than the settlers could endure, and headed by Parson Shepherd, they hunted Randolph to Boston, and made it desirable for that individual to look elsewhere for a summer residence. From that day to this Nahant has continued to be the queen of seaside resorts, but the later invasions from Boston have been of a more peaceful and desirable character. So the century passed away, and gradually the turmoils of its later years subsided, and the lives of the people moved on in straighter lines. In 1712 Lynnfield was set off as a separate town, and two years later a meeting-house was built. In all the early New England settlements the meeting-house was the center of influence and power. The building of a meeting-house and the settlement of a minister was insisted upon as a necessary preliminary to the recognition of a new municipality. If law and public policy could have made a people as a whole religious and God-fearing, our ancestors would have been entitled to canonization. Possibly some of them are, for what they did accomplish.

Farming continued to be the chief occupation of the settlers. There were a few tanneries, and in 1760 the manufacture of shoes had begun to receive considerable attention. Some skilled workmen in the line of ladies' shoes had come to the town from England, and they had imparted their skill to the home workmen, so that in 1764 The Boston Gazette records the fact that " the women's shoes made at Lynn do now exceed those usually imported, both in strength and beauty, but not in price" — a standard always since lived up to — and in 1768 it is stated that 80.000 pairs of shoes were made in Lynn the previous year. The foundation of our subsequent prosperity was then laid. Good work at a fair price was the motto. and in all the achievements of the later years this has been the governing principle.

The occurrences which led up to the War of the Revolution were full of interest and excitement for the citizens of Lynn. No less than the Bostonians did they resent the oppressions and exactions of the English Government. Some of her citizens participated in the Boston tea-party, and all joined with spirit and faithfulness in the crusade which was declared against all taxed tea.

SKETCH ON WALNUT STREET.

At a meeting on the 16th of December, 1773, it was, among other things, resolved, " That we highly disapprove of the landing and selling of such teas in America, and will not suffer any teas, subjected to a parliamentary duty, to be landed or sold in this town ; and that we stand ready to assist our brethren in Boston or elsewhere, whenever our aid shall be required, in repelling all attempts to land or sell any teas poisoned with a parliamentary duty."

There is little occasion to question the meaning of this declaration, and the people were as good as their word. It became known that Mr. James Bowler, on Water Hill, had a quantity of tea in store. A committee of ladies immediately waited upon him, demanded the tea, and destroyed it. The independent spirit of the mothers has been transmitted to their descendants, and the actors in this first American boycott planted seeds which still flourish in our soil. Holmes asserts that

> "The waters of the rebel bay
> Have kept their tea-leaf savor;
> Our old North Enders in their spray
> Still taste a Hyson flavor."

And the same spirit which led our ancestors to unite to resist an arbitrary and unjust tax still bands our people together to combat any real or fancied attempt at oppression.

The following year the port of Boston was closed, by order of the English Government. Then the storm clouds rapidly gathered. The people of Lynn made common cause with those of the surrounding towns. Couriers constantly

passed back and forth between Concord, Salem and Boston, and a company of
Lynn minute men assisted at the reception given the English regulars at Lexington — four of whom were killed in the fight, and several more were wounded.
Among the latter was Timothy Munroe, who had one ball through his leg, and
thirty-two bullet-holes through his clothes and hat.   Active measures were taken
for carrying on the war, which all now perceived was inevitable.   A Committee of Safety, consisting of Rev. John Treadwell, pastor of the First Church,
and Rev. Joseph Roby, of the Lynnfield parish, and Deacon Daniel Mansfield,
was appointed.   Guards were stationed on Sagamore Hill, Shepard street, and
the crossing at the Saugus River, and no one was suffered to pass out of town
without permission.   Arms were carried to meeting on the Sabbath, and it is
recorded that the minister appeared with his powder-horn under one arm and
his sermon under the other, and stood his musket at one side of the pulpit when
he rose to begin the service.   A company of minute men was formed, which
took part in the battle of Bunker Hill.   In the long and terrible war which followed, Lynn furnished her quota of men and means, and bore with patriotic
fortitude the privations, hardships and disappointments of that trying time.
One hundred and sixty-eight of her citizens were in the Continental Army, of
whom fifty-two men were lost, besides the four men killed at Lexington.

The years succeeding the war were devoted to retrieving the losses and
repairing the waste of that long struggle.   With the exception of the ripple
caused by Shay's Rebellion in 1787, there were no clouds in the political hori-
zon until 1808, when the Embargo brought all sorts of commercial activity to a
standstill, and reduced all manufacturing interests to a low ebb.   A majority of
the people were Democrats, and upheld the General Government in its policy,
though not without a vigorous protest from their Federalist neighbors.   Again,
in 1812, the naval war with England seriously checked all business for a time.
As was their wont, the citizens of Lynn were alive to the contest.   A privateer
was fitted out, which sent home three prizes, and generally the feelings of the
people were keyed up to the fighting pitch.   The frequent successes of the
Yankee tars and their impromptu fleet had caused the people to regard them as
well-nigh invincible.   One of the songs of the day ran :

> "I often have been told
> That the British seamen bold
> Could beat the tars of France so neat and handy O.
> But they never found their match
> Till the Yankees did them catch,
> For the Yankee tars for fighting are the dandy O.

It was, therefore, with great expectation of a glorious victory that the people
lined the heights of Nahant on the first day of June, 1813, to witness the battle
between the British ship Shannon and the American brig Chesapeake.   They
were doomed to a bitter disappointment, for after a short and spirited contest
Capt. Lawrence of the Chesapeake fell, her colors were lowered, and the people
sadly watched the Shannon depart with her prize for Halifax.

At last the treaty of peace brought an end to hostilities, and the people
once again turned their attention to their ordinary peaceful pursuits.   Farming
and shoemaking continued the chief occupations of the people.   Attempts were

made, from time to time, to inaugurate other industries, but either the place or the people were not suited to them. Several tanneries were in operation from 1820 to 1830, but by 1833 these were all discontinued, it being possible to purchase leather in Philadelphia cheaper than it could be manufactured here. In 1819 the sea-serpent made a reconnaisance of our shores, much to the consternation of the people, and in 1824 a visit from General Lafayette was the occasion of a great demonstration. Five years later the community was convulsed by the anti-masonry excitement, and for several years the opponents of that ancient order held complete control of municipal affairs. Scarcely had the public interest in this controversy begun to die away when abolition became a burning question. In the early days many slaves had been owned in Lynn, but at the opening of the Revolution all that were then held here were given their freedom. From that time onward there had been a marked and oftentimes outspoken opposition to the institution of slavery among the people, and in 1832 the Lynn Anti-Slavery Society was formed. This organization soon became noted for its advanced opinions, and its boldness in expressing them. Frequent meetings and discussions were held, and the silvery voice of Phillips and the burning eloquence of Garrison were often heard here in behalf of the southern slave.

Old Town Hall was frequently the scene of exciting occurrences, but probably no more spirited gathering ever met within its walls than was called together on the 5th of October, 1850, the occasion being the passage by Congress of the Fugitive Slave Law. The measure was denounced in the most unsparing manner, and those who had taken prominent part in the enactment of the law were called by name

OLD TOWN HALL.

and roundly castigated. The resolutions adopted by the meeting were characteristic of our people, and breathed the uncompromising hatred of oppression and love of liberty which, seventy-five years before, had led their fathers into rebellion. Following is one of the resolutions adopted at the meeting, which shows the temper of the people:

Resolved, That, since God hath commanded us to "bewray not him that wandereth," and since, our fathers being witnesses, every man's right to liberty is self-evident, we see no way of avoiding the conclusion of Senator Seward, that "it is in violation of the divine law to surrender the fugitive slave who takes refuge at our firesides;" and in view of this, as well as the notorious fact that the slave power has constantly trampled under foot the Constitution of the United States to secure its own extension or safety, and especially of the open, undisguised and acknowledged contempt of that instrument with which the slave states kidnap our colored citizens travelling south and imprison our colored seamen, we, in obedience to God's law, and in self-defense, declare that, Constitution or no Constitution, law or no law, with jury trial or without, the slave who has once breathed the air and touched the soil of Massachusetts shall never be dragged back to bondage.

Other large meetings were held in various parts of the Commonwealth, and such a fire of indignation was kindled that a Legislature was chosen which made such provisions that the operation of the law was seriously obstructed, and Massachusetts nullification became the theme of many a fiery Southern orator.

It was on Fayette street where Edmund Ingalls built his humble cottage, in the shade of some of the old giants of the forest. A small natural clearing formed the beginnings of his husbandry, and the sweet waters of Lake Wenuchus supplied both his family and his flocks. This cot long since gave way to a more pretentious edifice, and the outlines of the farm have been lost in the network of streets which compose that section of the city. It is two centuries since the sturdy Puritan sought repose in the bosom of his foster-mother. Lynn would doubtless have been sought out and settled, had not Edmund Ingalls first selected this as the place of his abode; but who shall say how much of our present permanence and prosperity we owe to the steady courage and fervent piety of our first citizen, whose blood has flowed down through successive generations in an ever-widening stream until, in our own day, his name is borne by half a hundred of our citizens? It was on the corner of Essex and Chestnut streets that John Wood built his modest dwelling. His house was long since demolished and his farm sub-divided, but his name became engrafted upon the locality which will be known as Woodend as long as Lynn continues a city. Joseph Armitage, who came here in 1630, cleared a farm on the north side of the Common. his land extending from Mall street to Strawberry Brook. The Common was then a forest and somewhat swampy, with a shallow brook crossing it. Mr. Armitage afterward opened the Anchor Tavern, situated in Saugus. on the carriage road to Boston. For one hundred and seventy years this was the most celebrated hostelry in Essex County. and it counted among its guests many of the noted men of the time. Another of the early settlers whose name has become inseparably connected with the city was Allen Breed, or Bread, as the custom of that early time had it. His farm was on Summer street, near the Western Avenue, and from him that section was early known as Breed's End. Samuel Graves, whose possessions lay west of the Floating Bridge. is the third of the Lynn immortals, that locality being yet called Gravesend,

SOUTHWEST SIDE OF MARKET STREET IN 1820.

though modern usage is gradually changing this to the more musical Glenmere. In 1836 it is mentioned that there were only seventeen buildings of brick in

SOUTHWEST SIDE OF MARKET STREET IN 1820.

Lynn, and only six of any material above two stories in height. The dwellings throughout the town had an average value of $500. These buildings were scattered along sixty streets, and not near enough together but that each family had plenty of breathing space. Market street was largely given up to dwellings, though here and there a shoe shop or tannery gave variety to the scene. The cuts on this and the preceding page give a faithful picture of Market street as it was in 1820. Referring to the numbers, 1 is now Sea street, 2 Timothy Alley, 3 Wm. Richards, 4 Viall's slaughter-house, 5 F. S. & H. Newhall's morocco factory, 6 Winthrop Newhall's tannery, 7 water trough, 8 Benj. Alley, 9 and 10 Solomon Alley, 11 Richard Pratt, 12 Pelatiah Purington, 13 John Alley, Jr., 14 now Summer street, 15 James Alley, 16 Simeon Breed, 17 Dr. Lummus, 18 Capt. Jos. Mudge, 19 Jerusha Williams, 20 and 21 Stephen Smith's house and shoe shop, 22 Gamaliel W. Oliver's shoe shop and house — in this shop William Lloyd Garrison worked shoemaking for some time — 23 J. B. Ingalls, 24 Rev. Enoch Mudge, 25 Methodist meeting-house, "The Bowery," now Lee Hall. These cuts were made from reliable data, and are said by those who survive that time to be a correct representation of things as they were then. The only building of that time now standing is close by the railroad. It is not shown in the cut, being on the opposite side of the street. It was then used as a morocco factory, and close by it was a creek through which the tides flowed in and out of what is now Harrison Court. A stone culvert spanned this stream just below where now the railroad crossing is.

Up to this time the town had probably not changed very much in the matter of its streets for a century or more. In the center of the town it had Market street, Liberty street, Spruce street — now a part of Washington — Sea street. Front street — now that part of Broad from Exchange to Market — Union street, Pine street — now Exchange — Spring street, Broad street. Further east were Broad, Nahant, Lewis, Chestnut, Fayette, Olive,

Mason, Orange, Essex, Pearl and High streets.   In the western part of the
town were Pleasant, Shepard, Summer, Commercial, Elm, North and South
Common, Franklin and Franklin avenue, Turnpike — now Western avenue —
Boston, North Shepard, Mall, Center and Federal streets.   Nahant street led to
Nahant over the beach; there being no road, the tides were watched to know
when the long beach could be used for travel.   Lewis street led to Swampscott
and into Humphrey street, and a cart road extended on through the farms to
Marblehead.   Essex street led from Woodend to Salem, with no cross streets.
All other parts of Lynn were in wood or pasture lands, or farms, and there
was no house south of Nahant and Broad streets, nor east of Nahant, Broad
and Lewis streets.   The lands between Lewis, Fayette and Essex streets, also
between Essex, Orange, Chestnut and the Turnpike, also south of Summer and
Commercial streets, were used as farms or pastures.   Around the southwest

OLD ANCHOR TAVERN.

corner of Union and Exchange streets ran a stone wall, and on the opposite
corner stood the Keene homestead.   Through a culvert under what is now
Central square flowed a stream of pure, cool water, from springs under the
present Central Station.   It formed a muddy, grassy brook which ran down
Union street to where the Ingalls building now is, then turned and flowed
through the gardens of Jonathan Connor and William D. Thompson, across
Broad street to the sea.   In the brook near Earl's new building was sunk a tub,
where the neighbors watered their cows.   Nearly all the principal families
owned a cow, and if they had no pasture, they hired or owned what was called
a " cow lease," or right to pasture a cow in Rocks Pasture or on Nahant.
Where Goldthwait's stable now is was a hill, on the summit of which was a

two-story house, the cellar of which must have been much above the roof of the present stable. Half-way down the hill was an old-fashioned well, with curb, sweep and an old oaken bucket. The stone wall extended up the south side of Union street for a short distance to the house of Farmer Silsbee, where Welch & Cummings' store now is. The one-story house of George Todd stood opposite Pearl street. From this point the stone wall extended most of the way to Woodend. A stone wall marked the site of the Sagamore House, and from Pearl street a wall extended nearly to the burying-ground. Where the East Baptist Church is, and beyond, was called Smith's field, and where Ireson street is was called Quaker Pasture — a decided contrast to the modern, busy, thronging Union street. There were no Beach, Baltimore, Atlantic, Ocean, or other cross streets in that section, nor any Silsbee, Green, Ireson, Rockaway, Washington, Willow, Munroe, Oxford, Andrew or Johnson streets, and only five or six cross streets from the Common. There were formerly salt works near the foot of S. N. Breed's wharf, with a windmill to pump the water into tanks for evaporation; and where the engine-house is was a small beach called "Water Side." Where Central avenue and Willow street are was a cow pasture, and Almont street was given over to brick-yards. At the foot of Nahant street was a fence, with a gate, to keep the cows from returning home too early.

The last decade of this period of our history is full of events of great importance as bearing on the future of the town. First, in 1838, came the Eastern Railroad, pushing its way north and east — first to Salem, and then onward toward Portland. The projectors of the railroad were men of courage and foresight. The science of railroad building and management, as it is now understood, was an unknown quantity, and the tremendous possibilities of the steam locomotive undreamed of. They came to Lynn, and calling the prominent business men together, asked their opinion as to the average number of passengers they might expect between Lynn and Boston. After mature deliberation and close calculation, the conclusion was reached that the average might reach thirty-eight per day, though one gentleman emphatically dissented, saying that "never in the world will they have so many!" The first station

FIRST RAILROAD STATION IN LYNN.

was a one-story wooden structure, about forty feet long, with a bell on the roof, which was rung on the arrival of each train. The first cars were about fifteen feet long, and seated twenty-two persons. The first locomotives were very crude, and had scarcely power enough to draw the few coaches in the train. Frequently in cold weather, or when facing a high wind across the marshes, the trains would be compelled to stop to get a head of steam sufficient to proceed. That was railroading under difficulties. But with the railroad came new life and energy into the place, which made itself manifest in the impetus given to business and the various new enterprises which sprung into life. The financial panic of the previous year, though falling heavily upon many of our manufacturers, had served to clear the business atmosphere, and brought many young men to the front. The era of invention, which has astonished the world by its productions, was then just beginning, and the shoemaking industry early began to receive its share of attention. A few minor inventions were brought out prior to 1850, but they were mostly crude and of little use; but they began to open the way for the great revolution in the methods of shoe manufacture which began ten years later. They consisted chiefly in improvements in lasts, and in methods of cutting the soles. The styles of boots most commonly made had been foxed gaiters, slippers and buskins, but in 1848 the congress boot was invented, which at once came into great favor. The city, in the years 1840 to 1850, took rapid strides both in population and business, and it began to be felt that Lynn had outgrown her town organization. The subject of obtaining a city charter was agitated for several years. Finally, on the 10th of April, 1850, the Legislature granted a charter, and on the 19th it was accepted by the town. With this action may be said to end the second period of our history. In our brief review we have seen a sparsely-settled colony, planted in a wilderness, grow to a busy and prosperous town, with an industry of sufficient magnitude to give employment to thousands of busy workers, and prosperous in a marked degree.

RED ROCK, LYNN BEACH.

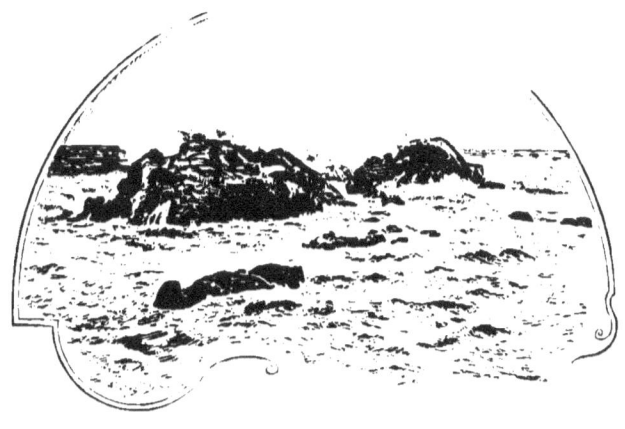

Lynn Legends.

THE legendary history of Lynn forms one of its most fascinating chapters. The limits of this work prevent more than the briefest reference to some of the more important of these events, although in number and interest they would suffice for a separate volume; and these naturally find a place where the sketches of the town end and those of the city begin. The pathetic tale of the Bridal of Pennacook reaches farthest back into the shadowy vista of the past—

"A story of the marriage of the chief
Of Saugus to the dusky Weetamoo,
Daughter of Passaconaway, who dwelt
In the old time upon the Merrimack."

The story, in brief, is that Winnepurkit, as Morton has it, or, more properly, Winnepoyekin, son of Nanapashemet, sagamore of Saugus, when he came to man's estate, made choice, for his wife, of the daughter of Passaconaway, the great chieftain of the tribes inhabiting the Merrimack valley. Passaconaway was not only a mighty chieftain, but, if we may believe the early English chronicles of his doings, he was the most accomplished wizard the New World ever knew. These learned and reverend writers gravely assert that, so skilled was he in the arts of necromancy, he could cause a green leaf to grow in winter, trees to dance, water to burn, and numberless things of a like marvellous nature, through his mystical invocations. The union of the young people was blessed by the great chieftain, and in due time Weetamoo was seated in her lord's wigwam on Sagamore Hill, with the broad bay spread out before her door, now shining like a burnished mirror in the sun, and then rolling its angry waves upon the beach in thunderous monotone, or dashing them upon the rocks of Little Nahant. Before long, however, a homesick longing for a sight of her father filled her heart, and like a kind husband, Winnepurkit sent her home, escorted by some of his most mighty men. The daughter was received with open arms, and the escort were cordially entertained and graciously dismissed. After a short stay she signified a desire to return to her noble husband, upon which her father sent messengers to Winnepurkit to notify him of the desire of his wife, and to request the Saugus sachem to dispatch a suitable guard to escort his wife back through the wilderness to her home. But here an unexpected difficulty arose, for Winnepurkit curtly told the messengers to carry word to his father-in-law, " That when his wife departed from him he caused his own men to wait upon her to her father's territories, as did become him ; but now that she had an intent to return, it did become her father to send her back with a convoy of his own people." Both were men of high spirit, and neither would yield, and so the poor princess was forced to remain with her father, at least for a time. Tradition has it, however, that her woman's wit found a way through or around the difficulty, and that she, after a while, made her way back to her husband's home. Whittier, however, gives a different and tragic ending to the tale. In his poem, the heart-broken Bride of Pennacook determines to return alone. She steals away from her attendant maidens, launches her frail canoe upon the swollen and threatening Merrimac, and is instantly swept

> " Down the vexed center of that rushing tide,
> The thick, huge ice blocks threatening either side,
> The foam-white rocks of Amoskeag in view,
> With arrowy swiftness —
>
> Down the white rapids like a sere leaf whirled,
> On the sharp rocks and piled-up ices hurled.
> Empty and broken, circled the canoe
> In the vexed pool below, but where was
> Weetamoo ? "

THE PIRATES' GLEN.

About the year 1656, in the twilight of a pleasant evening, a strange vessel was seen to approach the shore off the mouth of the Saugus River, where she furled her sails and dropped anchor. When the shades of night had fallen, a boat was lowered, and four men rowed silently up the river to where it emerges from the hills. There they landed and turned into the woods. The strange visitors doubtless thought themselves unobserved, but those were perilous times, and sharp eyes had followed them. Many were the conjectures occasioned by these unusual movements. The next morning the settlers rose early to learn more of these unannounced visitors, but the stranger-vessel had disappeared, and no trace either of her or her singular crew could be found. The occurrence was a nine days' wonder among the settlers, but the interest had nearly died out when one day a workman at the Iron Works found a paper lying in a conspicuous place, running to the effect that if a certain quantity of shackles, handcuffs, and other articles named, were made and deposited with secrecy in a certain place in the woods, an amount of silver equal to their value would be found in their stead. The articles were made and deposited as directed, and on the following morning they had been taken away, and the money left as agreed upon. Some months later the four men returned, and selected one of the most secluded spots in the woods of Saugus for their abode ; and interest is added to the tale by the statement that the pirate chief brought with him a beautiful woman. The place of their retreat was a narrow valley shut in on two sides by craggy, precipitous rocks, and screened on the other by a thick growth of evergreens. The spot was admirably chosen for concealment and observation as well, for from the cliff on the eastern side of this glen a noble expanse of country and sea, stretching far toward the south, is spread before the eye. Here the pirates built themselves a small hut, and here it is said that the chief's beautiful mistress sickened and died. After a time the retreat of the pirates became noised abroad. Three of them were captured and taken to England, where they suffered the penalty of their crimes upon the gibbet. The fourth, Thomas Veale, escaped, and for many years thereafter made his home in a cave in the woods, which the band had previously utilized as a storehouse for their treasures. Here he practiced the trade of a shoemaker, occasionally visiting the village to obtain food.

ASCENT TO DUNGEON ROCK.

In 1658 an earthquake shook up the settlers in a most alarming manner. The entire face of Dungeon Rock was split off, and the cavern forever closed up. The legend has it that the pirate was entombed therein, with all his treasures, and possibly one of the village girls who had mysteriously disappeared some months previous. A realistic turn was given to the legend by the declaration of a certain Joel Dunn, that on the night of the earthquake, during the tremendous storm which raged, he got lost in the woods at the north of the town, and in his wanderings found himself, at the dead of night, at the door of the cavern. He entered, and found the pirate working by the light of a blazing pine knot. Newhall gives a lifelike picture of their interview, which waxed as stormy as the weather outside, and the pirate had just grasped his visitor by the throat, when the earthquake shock came. Just how it came about is not explained, but somehow Joel was not included in the general destruction which followed, but was found next morning in a sad state by men from the settlement who, alarmed by his non-appearance the night before, had set out to search for him. When he had recovered he told his wonderful story, which naturally occasioned much wonderment; but while the people seemed willing to believe the pirate Veale was entombed beneath Dungeon Rock, even the grave Mr. Whiting felt constrained to say that while he had no doubt that Joel Dunn passed the night on which the earthquake occurred, in the woods, it was most likely that a large jug which Joel had taken into the woods had been the inspiration of his wonderful visions. The treasures thus believed to be buried in the heart of Dungeon Rock have never been exhumed, but about forty years since, Hiram Marble, under the direction of spirit mediums, began the search for it. For more than a quarter of a century father and son toiled early and late to unlock the secret caverns of the cliff, and when they were ready to abandon the work, they were again spurred on by some new delusive revelation of the spirits. And even when death had released the elder enthusiast from his delusion, the son carried on the work as the most sacred of trusts until he, too, died in the same fatal delusion.

ENTRANCE TO DUNGEON ROCK CAVE.

A visit to Dungeon Rock is full of interest, not only on account of the traditions which surround the locality, but for the natural beauties which are revealed on every side. Two miles out from the city, in the heart of the Lynn forest, few wilder or more picturesque spots can be found in New England, and one can hardly realize that he is scarcely out of sight and sound of the homes and mart of nearly fifty thousand people. The ledge on one side is a sheer precipice ; the other side. which the road ascends, is less abrupt, and is covered with a grove of oak trees, growing among enormous boulders, with which, in fact, the whole region abounds. The cave which once existed in the ledge was

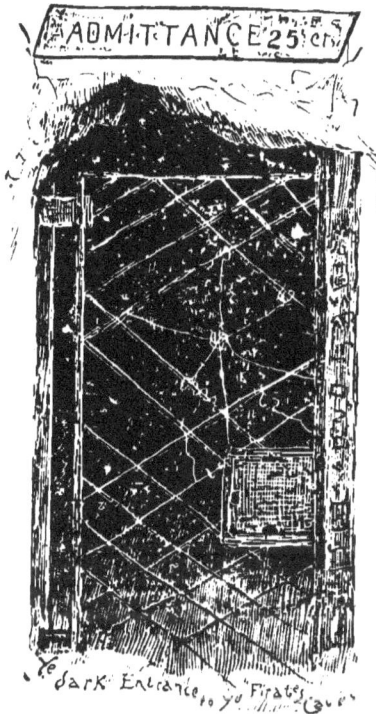

closed by the great earthquake — to doubt the legend, with the evidences all around you, would be folly — and some avaricious vandal has blown out the remains of the entrance in the vain hope of finding out the well-kept secret of the cliff. The entrance to the excavation made by the Marbles. father and son. is barred by a grating. not specially suggestive of aught piratical. or in any way uncanny, the open sesame to which is a quarter in hand, paid to the pleasant appearing lady, sister of the younger Marble, who is now the presiding genius of the locality. The key turns with a creak in the rusty lock, and the door opens outward with a groan. The descent into the tunnel is first by a series of rickety steps, then by such foothold as one is fortunate enough to gain on the slippery rock. The entire gallery is about one hundred and fifty feet in length, descending in its course some forty feet. On account, however, of the zig-zag direction which the often-amended revelations of the spirits marked out, the rock is not actually penetrated more than one hundred feet. The formation is porphyry, as hard as adamant, and without seam or break to indicate that a cavern ever existed there or thereabouts ; and one is compelled to the opinion that the spirits who directed the operations must have served their earthly apprenticeship in some of the wild-cat enterprises of the wild-west. But scarcely has our incredulity begun to assert it when it is again challenged by the production of the relics of the pirates found, so says our entertainer, tucked in cran-nies of the rock. The sheath looks as though it had done hard service, and the knife has a suffi-ciently piratical, blood-thirsty appearance to suit the most fastidious. What is left of the scissors has a more modern look. but the old anvil brings us back to the days of hard, practical things. For no matter how legend and story may people the rocks and grottoes of the neighborhood with strange personages and shapes. or fill the hollows of the cliff with shining gold and precious gems and jewels ; regardless wholly of the phantom guides who promise to show the path to the hidden treasures ; the old anvil brings us to a realization of the fact that the path can be gained by mortals, and the treasures secured, only by hard blows with material implements. Judging from the nature of the rock, both father and son must have spent fully as much time at the anvil as in the tunnel. After all, the

history of the experiences of the Marbles in search of the hidden treasure of Dungeon Rock reads much like the story of most lives. Always almost within reach of the coveted blessing ; convinced that one more strong effort will bring it within their grasp ; disappointed and thwarted again and again, yet still buoyed with hope that success will come—how many have lived their day and gone to their rest with their dearest expectation unrealized ! But there is no time for moralizing. So, thanking our guide for her attention, we return to Lynn thoroughly satisfied with our excursion, and more than ever in love with Lynn and her surroundings.

THE TREASURE OF PINES POINT.

There has ever been a peculiar interest attaching to tales of wonder or adventure wherein pirates and their exploits form an important element. The New World, with its many unexplored bays and safe harbors, which had so hospitably received the early settlers, was supposed by them to be also in high favor, as a safe rendezvous, with the black-haired, blood-thirsty gentry who roamed the seas, collecting tribute of all nations. Upon our headlands they set their watch, and held high revelry after their successful ventures. Their methods of making money were not so gentlemanly or refined as those of some of our modern financiers, but were quite as honest, and the banks of deposit which they selected have never failed, nor their cashiers taken vacations in the penitentiary or Canada. Had Capt. Kyd endowed all the localities with which tradition has credited him, his wealth must have been marvellously great, and his methods a step in advance of any system of stock watering or manipulation since devised. Longfellow has invested the old stone tower of Newport with a halo of romance. Thither, says his Skeleton in Armor,

> "Three weeks we westward bore,
> And when the storm was o'er,
> Cloud-like we saw the shore
>   Stretching to leeward;
> There, for my lady's bower,
> Built I the lofty tower
> Which, to this very hour,
>   Stands looking seaward."

The fact that this tower was built by the first settlers and used as a windmill detracts nothing from the interest of the legend, and it is possible that many, if not most, other legends which tell of mysterious visitations of pirates and secreting of treasure which they never came to reclaim have as slender a foundation as the instance named. Nevertheless, in the time when the Old Anchor Tavern, or the "Blew Ankor." as its early title was, constituted the half-way house between Boston and Salem, and around whose crackling fire the travellers and idlers used to meet to exchange yarns, there was a belief held by many that the pirate crew, whose craft so mysteriously appeared off the mouth of the Saugus River, had buried a chest of gold beneath a flat stone at the roots of a tree at Pines Point, as it was then known. On many a dark night might the solitary treasure-seeker have been seen groping among the trees with his lantern and spade, vainly searching for the hidden doubloons, but the barren point would not give up its secret.

But one night a party was made up at the Anchor Tavern to make a final search for the coveted treasure. Newhall, in his Jewels of the Third Plantation, gives the only account of this enterprise we have seen. The night agreed upon was fair, and a

bright moon shed her favoring beams upon them. David Kunkshamooshaw, a mighty wizard, and skilled with the divining rod, was one of the party. They made the journey to the point in the early evening. The action of the hazel rods in the hands of David was satisfactory in the extreme. Then he proceeded, with his incantations, to charm away the evil spirits, who, he solemnly averred, would combine to prevent them from accomplishing their object, and a circle was drawn around the spot where the hazel rods had indicated the treasure was concealed, over which the spirits could not go to do them injury. He then charged them not to utter a word, even in whispers, for if they did, their whole labor would come to naught, though by keeping within the ring they might escape bodily harm. The work then began, and in due time they came upon the flat stone which they knew covered the treasure-chest. Just as they began working around it, there came a tremendous gust of wind sweeping down over the beach with such fury that they were nearly blown from their feet and outside the circle. But they recovered from their momentary fright, and resumed operations. A stout lever was adjusted, and they were just giving a vigorous heave at the stone, when an astounding neigh, as of a horse on the very bound of the circle, sounded in their ears. The lever dropped from their grasp, but as they peered around nothing could be seen, and at the word from David, who constantly perambulated the circle, making wild gesticulations, they again plied the lever, and the ponderous stone began to move from its bed. Soon the edge was high enough so that one of them, holding down his lantern and peering eagerly into the darkness beneath, declared he saw the corner of the long-sought-for iron chest. This stimulated them to renewed effort, and in a moment more their dreams would have been fulfilled, but a most astounding circumstance occurred, which is told in the graphic language of Judge Newhall :

" At that critical moment there came another awful gust of wind, but this time from over the water, saturating their clothing with salt spray, almost blinding them, and setting everything whirling again. Then was heard the heavy tread of a rapidly advancing horse. On, on, he dashed, in headlong fury, out into the moonlight — a gigantic courser, with flaring tail erect and long mane waving and curling in the breeze ; snorting and prancing in the most threatening manner. Astride his back, without saddle or bridle, hatless, and with hair streaming in lank locks about his shoulders, sat a man of giant form and graceless mein, a hideous grin playing about his toothless mouth. On, on he rushed with unabated fury, directly toward the petrified group. But the instant he reached the charmed circle his progress was arrested. Not a hoof could pass the magic bound ; the desperate rearings, plungings and snortings of the horse, nor the fiery glaring and spurring of the rider, could avail. But in that alarming attitude of affairs the affrighted diggers could not continue their work, and their tools fell from their paralyzed hands. Things remained thus for some minutes ; and then began a frantic race around the circle, the distance narrowing at every turn. Just on the verge the furious beast wheeled and reared and plunged, as if determined to dash across in spite of fate itself. David now for the first time showed signs of terror. With fiery eyes and hissing breath the fiery steed poised himself on his hind feet, while his rider in stentorian voice vociferated : ' By my blood, what do ye here? ye are well set to work filching my gold, hard earned upon the sea by dagger and by fire. But the devil will yet save his own, I wot. Aroynt ye, or bear a pirate's malediction.' The ponderous hoofs were quivering almost directly over the head of David, who had stepped forth to see there was no break in the ring, when, thrown suddenly off his guard, with trembling lips he gave utterance to a propitiatory ejaculation in these imploring words of his euphonious native tongue :—ahquonlamannean nummatchescongask ; poliquohwussinnean. In an instant, down came the hoofs, almost upon his head ; and then rang the exulting laugh of the rider out over the sea ; and the wild neigh of the horse was louder still. The spell was broken and there was no longer a charm-protected bound. They pranced within the ring without restraint ; the stone fell back over the chest ; the affrighted diggers scattered for dear life. The triumphant horse and his rider, having accomplished their purpose, sped off among the trees, the one whinnying and the other laughing till the old woods resounded with the weird clamor."

This was enough. Treasure-seeking at the point became unpopular, and there is no record of any subsequent attempt to locate or unearth the hidden treasure. There has been a great change in the appearance of the point and the surrounding marshes since that memorable night, but it may be a pleasant diversion some fine summer day to undertake to locate the spot where the chest of gold as really lies buried now as it ever did.

DREAD LEDGE, SWAMPSCOTT

The Quaker Invasion.

URING the first twenty-five years, the colonists of New England managed their affairs both civil and religious entirely in their own way, and doubtless much to their own satisfaction. Nearly, if not quite, all of those who came hither from England prior to the death of Charles Stuart did so to gain greater freedom in their religious opinions and practices. They came, many of them, from the best-educated, property-owning classes, who, being hindered from worshiping God according to the dictates of their consciences, at home, resolutely, and of their own accord, sought asylum in the New World. Under the royal patent, those named therein came into absolute control of the territory covered by it, subject only to the claims of the aboriginal proprietors, and the several towns acquired a like title under the grants from the original patentees.

Matters of religion, especially the organization of a church and the settlement of a minister, became questions of immediate concern, for it was because of their religion, and their regard for their religious teachers, that they had left their former pleasant homes to end their days in the wilderness. Matters of purely civil administration received only secondary attention during the early years of the colony, being, for the most part, provided for in the administration and organization of the church. What seems to us a strange and unreasonable regulation, because of the changed circumstances of our time, that everyone should be taxed for the support of the church, and that no one should vote who was not a church member, was the natural thing for them to do, because ninety-nine persons out of every hundred were members of the church. The charter of the colony in no respect resembled the Constitution under which we live; it was, on the contrary, that of a trading company — a close corporation which had the technical right to expel any person whose presence was deemed prejudicial to the interests of the company in general. Having been persecuted for their religion at home, they naturally sought, in establishing their own religious system, to throw around it every safeguard and influence to maintain its suprem-

acy and secure its permanence Their troubles at home had arisen from a con-
flict of beliefs ; therefore they would prevent a recurrence of similar troubles in
their new home by shutting the door tight against all who would not unreserv-
edly subscribe to their system.

Their plan was, in a certain narrow and technical sense, just, and would
doubtless have been a good one if it could have been made to work. The obstacle to its success lay in their inability to control the thoughts and consciences
of all their own people, and the extent of their coast line, which precluded
perfect police supervision of all new-comers. The obstacles were not at first
apparent, and where there was such a will to carry out their ideas, with a man
like Gov. Endicott in authority, seconded by an exceptionally able Court of
Assistants, there was certain to be devised ways and means.

The events attending upon the preaching of George Fox, and the methods
by which the English authorities attempted to check the new religious movement, had not been unnoted in the Massachusetts colony ; and with a singular
seeming forgetfulness of the trials they themselves had passed through, the
English Puritans were quite as fierce in their denunciations of the new sect as
the authorities of the Establishment, and lent ready countenance to the persecution which was at once raised against it. And the Massachusetts authorities
were in full sympathy with their English cousins in regarding Quakerism as a
dangerous heresy to be combatted by all means. The Friends on the other side
had endured enough persecution to raise the zeal of the leaders to the point of
enthusiasm, and it was not long before some of their number felt called to testify
for their faith in the New World.

The first Quakers of note to arrive in Boston were Mary Fisher and Ann
Austin. They came in 1652, though it appears that for two years several families of that faith had dwelt unmolested in the Plymouth colony, and that a few
had settled in Lynn and Salem. Both were women of mark, having suffered
imprisonment and scourging for their faith in England. They found the Massachusetts authorities ready to receive them. They were promptly imprisoned,
their books publicly burned, and by the first departing vessel were sent back to
England, the jailer keeping their beds and Bibles for his fees. Eight more who
subsequently arrived were similarly treated, and at the next session of the court
a law was enacted forbidding all masters of vessels from bringing Quakers into
this jurisdiction, and threatening any Friends who might come, with the House
of Correction. This had no effect to deter them from coming, but, on the contrary, only served to inflame the missionary zeal of the Quaker propagandists.
The following year a number of Friends, men and women, landed in Boston.
They received equally prompt attention as their predecessors, and several of
them were accorded the additional courtesy of twenty stripes on the bare back
with a whip of three cords, knotted at the ends to give point and pungency to
the proceedings. During the succeeding years the whipping-post was one of
the busiest of our public institutions. Some of those who had been sent away
having returned, the following order was issued by the Court :

"To the Marshall-General or his deputy : You are to take with you the
executioner, and repair to the House of Correction, and there see him cut off the
right ears of John Copeland, Christopher Holder and John Rouse, Quakers,

in execution of the sentence of the Court of Assistants, for the breach of the law entitled Quakers.

EDWARD RAWSON,
Secretary.

And the order was carried out to the letter; but even these harsh measures failed of the desired effect. Not only were the English Quakers stirred to greater zeal, but murmurings against the severity of the punishments began to be heard among the colonists, and it was found that many of them had adopted the Quaker belief, these being specially numerous in the vicinity of Lynn and Salem, so that the government had not only those who came hither to look after, but also an uncomfortable number planted upon the soil, who were every whit as firm in their faith as the magistrates in their determination to root out Quakerism. Lynn and Salem early became a center of the Quaker influence. Refusing to perform military service or to pay church rates, they suffered many indignities, and had their cattle, corn, hay and domestic furniture distrained for payment. Mention is made in the Friends' records of George Oaks, who appears to have been one of the first Quakers in Lynn, the entry being: "Taken away for the priest, Samuel Whiting, one cow, valued at £3." The good minister seems not to have despised the cow, though his estimate of the Quakers is given. In enumerating the evils with which the people of New England have to contend, he remarks that "it is cause for humiliation that our sins have exposed us to live among such wicked sinners," among whom he ranks "atheists and Quakers." It has been understood among Friends that the first Friends' meetings in this vicinity were held in a house on what is called the old road to Salem, and near the Lynn mineral spring farm; composed of those from Salem and Lynn who had adopted the Friends' belief. But while these things had been going on in Lynn, the authorities in Boston had no end of trouble. The whippings, imprisonments and maimings to which the Quakers were subjected at length roused the genuine martyr spirit in not a few, who felt that they could render no better service to their religion than to come to New England and protest against the persecutions of their sect. Accordingly in 1658 the General Court passed a law banishing all incoming Quakers "on pain of death." This severe legislation was not passed unanimously. Very many of the Court had begun to doubt the wisdom of the course that was being pursued, and the measure had only a majority of one in a vote of twenty-five. The details for the enforcement of the statute included summary arrest and imprisonment without bail until the next term of Court. Scarcely was the ink dry on the parchment when William Robinson and Marmaduke Stevens, with Mary Dyer and Nicholas Davis, arrived in Boston. They were arrested, and a decree of banishment issued against them. The two latter obeyed for a time, but Robinson and Stevens came directly to Lynn and Salem, where they commenced active evangelistic work. But the authorities soon learned their whereabouts, and they were re-arrested. The following month Mary Dyer returned boldly to Boston, and was immediately secured. In due season the fated trio were taken before the Court, tried, and sentence of death passed upon them. On the 27th of October they were led away to execution. Robinson and Stevens were hanged first, but as the rope was being adjusted about the neck of Mary Dyer, a reprieve was received, and she was sent to her home in Rhode Island. The next summer found her again in Boston. She was taken before the Court, and the sentence reaffirmed. Being asked why she had returned, she said: " I came, in obedience to the will of God, to the last General Court, desiring you to repeal your unrighteous laws of banishment on pain of death; and that same is my work now, and earnest request; although I told you that if you refused to repeal them, the Lord would send others of His servants to witness against them." This time there was no reprieve, and she died at the time appointed.

The record of the months following reads little like the history of Puritan New England. It would be impossible to describe the bitterness of persecution to which Quakers in the northern counties of Massachusetts and in New Hampshire were subjected. To the terrors of the jail and the pillory were added unspeakable indignities at the hand of brutal officials. Both men and women were stripped of their clothing and cruelly scourged at the whipping-post, or were tied to a cart's tail and whipped from town to town, their property confiscated and their homes taken from them, and in some instances they were condemned to be sold for payment of jail and officers' fees. On one such episode Whittier has founded his famous poem of Cassandra Southwick, which

is in many respects one of the most thrilling products of his gifted pen. And not a few suffered death upon the gallows. A characteristic official document of the time reads thus:

" To the Constables of Boston, Charlestown, Malden and Lynn :

You are required to take into your custody, respectively, Edward Wharton, convicted of being a vagabond from his own dwelling place ; and the Constable of Boston is to whip him severely with thirty stripes on his naked body; and from constable to constable you are required to convey him until he come to Salem, the place where he saith he dwelleth; and in so doing this shall be your warrant.

JOHN ENDICOTT.

A sudden ending came to the bloody persecution. Prominent Friends in England succeeded in gaining the ear of Charles, who had but just been called back from his twelve years' exile. Reports had already reached the royal ear of the independent attitude assumed by the colonists, most of whom had been in ardent sympathy with Cromwell, and had not been backward in expressing their preferences; and the incident of the persecutions was seized upon as a convenient pretext for letting the colonists feel the weight of his hand. Accordingly a letter was addressed to Governor Endicott, under the King's hand, ordering the immediate cessation of the persecution; and, as if to make the intervention all the more galling, the letter was given into the hands of Samuel Shattuck, a Quaker who had but lately been expelled from Boston, to be conveyed to its destination. The incidents of the reception of this letter have inspired the pens of both Longfellow and Whittier. The verses of the latter are especially valuable as showing the estimate in which a member of the persecuted sect holds the character and acts of their greatest enemy in the New World:

THE KING'S MISSIVE.

Under the great hill sloping bare
    To cove and meadow and common lot,
In his council chamber and oaken chair
    Sat the worshipful Governor Endicott —
A grave, strong man who knew no peer
In the pilgrim land where he ruled in fear
Of God, not man, and for good or ill,
Held his trust with an iron will.

He had shorn with his sword the cross from out
    The flag, and cloven the may-pole down;
Harried the heathen round about,
    And whipped the Quakers from town to town.
Earnest and honest, a man at need
To burn like a torch for his own harsh creed,
He kept with the flaming brand of his zeal
The gate of the holy commonweal.
                *   *   *   *   *   *

The door swung open, and Rawson, the Clerk,
    Entered and whispered under breath:
"There waits below for the hangman's work
    A fellow banished on pain of death —
Shattuck of Salem, unhealed of the whip,
Brought over in Master Goldsmith's ship,
At anchor here in a Christian port,
With freight of the Devil and all his sort!"

Twice and thrice on his chamber floor
    Striding fiercely from wall to wall;
"The Lord do so to me and more,"
    The Governor cried, "if I hang not all!

Bring hither the Quaker!" Calm, sedate,
With the look of a man at ease with fate,
Into that presence grim and dread
Came Samuel Shattuck, with hat on head.

"Off with the knave's hat!" An angry hand
   Smote down the offence; but the wearer said,
With a quiet smile: "By the King's command,
   I bear his message and stand in his stead."
In the Governor's hand a missive he laid,
With the royal arms on its seal displayed;
And the proud man spake, as he gazed thereat,
Uncovering: "Give Mr. Shattuck his hat."

He turned to the Quaker, bowing low:
   "The King commandeth your friends' release;
Doubt not he shall be obeyed, although
   To his subject's sorrow and sin's increase.
What he here enjoineth John Endicott
His loyal servant questioneth not.
You are free! God grant the spirit you own
May take you from us to parts unknown."

So persecution ended, and the Quakers gradually came into possession of all the rights of citizens, and were accorded the privilege of churches and schools of their own. In Lynn the number of Quakers rapidly increased. The witchcraft delusion in 1692 diverted attention from them for a time, and after that had become history, they were found to have become somewhat aggressive and disputatious. Finally Rev. Mr. Shepherd hit upon a new method of combatting them, and a fast was appointed for the church, to the end "that the spiritual plague might proceed no further," of which Cotton Mather wrote: "The spirit of our Lord Jesus Christ gave a remarkable effect unto this holy method of encountering the charms of Quakerism. It proved a better method than any coercion of the civil magistrates." And he adds: "Quakerism in Lynn received, as I am informed, a death wound from that very day." However this may have been, eight years later we find the Rev. Mr. Shepherd, with an imported champion from England, meeting the leading lights of the Quakers in a joint discussion, which narrowly escaped being a riot. In 1723 Richard Estes presented the society with a large lot on Silsbee street, on which their first house of worship was erected. In 1816 that house was removed to make room for the present edifice, and now serves as an office for S. N. Breed & Co., on the corner of Broad and Beach streets. In 1826 the Quaker meeting-house in Boston and the burial grounds adjoining having been long disused, and few or none of the society remaining in the city, it was thought best to remove the bones; and the remains of one hundred and nine persons, among whom were many martyrs to the faith, were taken up and removed to the Friends' cemetery in this city. The neighborhood of Nahant street was for many years headquarters for the Society of Friends, and to this day their descendants own and occupy some of the best places in that beautiful section. This, in brief, is the story of the Quaker Invasion, and it forms one of the most remarkable chapters in the history of our city and of the Commonwealth.

The Witchcraft Tragedy.

THE clouds of superstition still hung heavily over humanity when the first homes were made in Massachusetts. The settlers had that faith in God which could support them through the dangers and trials attendant upon the establishment of a home in the wilderness. They had an equally vivid belief in the existence not only of Satan, but of an innumerable host of imps who waited upon him to do his bidding. The first voyagers who approached our shore reported that they " saw Indians and devils sitting upon the rocks;" the settlers, sitting in their homes in the evening with the doors and windows tightly barred, while the forest choirs raised their nocturnal anthems, could distinguish the voices of devils mingling with the bark of the fox, the howl of the wolf, and the scream of the catamount. And even Obadiah Turner, one of the brightest and steadiest lights of the community, credited Satan with personal attentions rendered. He tells his own story best:

" It was somewhat within ye night when we came in sight of home. In coming over ye hillock near ye doore of our habitation, I descried a daintie white rabbit, as yt seemed, wch I deemed would make a savory dish for breakfast on ye morrow. Giving chase, I was soon almost vpon him, when, lo, he whisked up a bushy tail over his hinder parts, and then threw it towards me with a mighty rush; and yt shed upon me a liquor of such stinke yt nothing but ye opening of ye bottomless pit can equal. My eyes were blinded, and my breath seemed stopped forever. When I recovered, ye smell remained vpon me, insomuch yt they would fain drive me from ye house, saying yt they could not abide within while I remained. And I still carry yt about with me in a yet terrible degree. I am persuaded yt is another device of Satan; yt four-footed beast being an impe let to do ye Devil his baptism by sprinkling."

Among a people thus ready to give the devil his due and more, it is little wonder that belief in witchcraft, which had held full sway in England and on the continent for two centuries, should be regarded almost as one of the tenets of their religion. Against an inherited superstition, reason and judgment are of little avail.

The popular idea of a witch was grotesque; the theory being that in the constant endeavor of Satan to win back to himself those souls who had been redeemed by the death of Christ and baptized, many, probably most, would be faithful to their vows and the church, in which case he had no power over them; but that occasionally an individual would be found, who, yielding to his wiles, entered into a written compact whereby, in exchange for their souls, they received certain specified powers to work evil, such as to raise storms, blast crops, render men and beasts barren, inflict racking pains upon an enemy or cause him to waste away in sickness; and an evil spirit was appointed as a special attendant, which most often took the form of a cat, but could transform itself at will into the likeness of any other animal. It was believed that Satan made his conquests in the form of a beautiful man or maiden, with whom vows of love were plighted, and that at certain stated times were held meetings of witches and their satanic lovers, called witches' sabbaths, to which they rode through the air seated comfortably astride of a broomstick, making their exit by the chimney and returning in the same manner; and having sold themselves to Satan, as good subjects they must continually strive to induce others to similarly dispose of themselves. But with all the power thus conferred upon the deluded mortal, they could not exercise it to better their own condition.

There were various methods of testing alleged witches, to ascertain if they were guilty of forbidden practices. One was, to confront them with their victims, and if the paroxysms or phenomena of the infliction were repeated, it was regarded as positive proof of guilt. Another method was, to search the body of the accused for the " devil's mark." When the compact with Satan was sealed, he was supposed to touch some part of the body, which at once lost the sense of touch. The delicate and humane method of finding this mark was to remove the witch's clothing, and examine every portion of the body, using sharp needles to locate the insensible part. Another method, and one which was deemed infallible, was to cast the accused into deep water. If she floated, it was infallible evidence of satanic assistance. If she sunk, she was as conclusively proved innocent; but the vindication usually came too late to be of much comfort to the accused. All these dark superstitions the settlers in these New England towns brought with them from England. For some years they had more tangible things to occupy their attention, but when the occasion served, the pent-up flames burst forth with redoubled fury.

In those early days the New England towns were more closely bound together in a common interest than now, and though the earliest outbreaks of the witchcraft mania took place in Boston and Salem, the people of Lynn were as profoundly stirred by them as the dwellers in the localities named. The first person to be denounced as a witch and arrested, condemned and executed was Margaret Jones of Charlestown, this occurring in 1648. Seven years later Mrs. Ann Hibbins, of Boston, was charged with witchcraft and condemned. Her case attracted widespread attention, and there were many dissenters from the severity of her sentence. The charge against her consisted chiefly in the allegation that she possessed a crabbed temper, and the original accusation was doubtless caused by personal spite. She was executed on Boston Common. From that time until 1692 there were occasional and widely separated accusations and trials for witchcraft, not enough to cause great popular excitement, but sufficient to keep alive the fire of superstition, ready to burst into flame when the occasion should serve.

The outbreak came in 1692, and so startlingly near our doors as to almost achieve the importance of a local event. Salem Village, now a portion of Danvers, is a quiet, unpretentious place, little suggestive of witchcraft or anything else so uncanny and weird. The quiet street still winds by the same old trees which stood there then, and the houses which were the homes of the principal actors in the bloody drama remain upon the old foundations. The parsonage was the scene of the first outbreak. Two children of the Rev. Samuel Parris were attacked with convulsions, and a black slave called Tituba was accused of having bewitched them, the accusation being made by a number of young girls who had been accustomed to meet at the parsonage at stated times during the winter. Tituba was promptly arrested, and in due course of justice put on trial. Nothing could be proved against her that would justify summary proceedings, and the principal excuse for holding her in jail for nine months were certain boastful claims made by her at her trial which have a

EXECUTION OF MRS. ANN HIBBINS.

strong suggestion of modern spiritualism. She was finally sold for payment of jail fees. The excitement caused by this occurrence soon rose to a frenzy. As though encouraged by their success in the case mentioned, the circle of girls soon after made accusation against well-known and hitherto respected residents of the surrounding country, and when confronted with the victims in court, the girls would calmly make the most preposterous statements of things done by the accused, which were accepted by the learned jurists of the day as competent evidence. Several of the accused persons, in order to save their lives, confessed to having signed their names in the Devil's book, to having been baptized by him, and to have attended midnight meetings of witches, or sacraments held on the green near the parsonage, to which they came riding through the air. They admitted that he had sometimes appeared to them in the form of a black dog or cat, sometimes in that of a horse, and once as "a fine, grave man," but generally as a black man of severe aspect. But many would not so confess, and suffered the penalty. The trials were the merest farce, the judgment apparently being made before the evidence was in. Thirteen women and five men were hung, and two — Rev. George Burroughs and Giles Corey — were pressed to death beneath heavy weights because they would neither confess nor plead to their accusations. More than one hundred others were accused and

THE PARSONAGE, SALEM VILLAGE.

imprisoned, of whom seven belonged in Lynn. Many of these persons were of advanced age, and the long months spent in Boston prison must have been a terrible hardship. It was a reign of terror indeed. No one was safe. The honored citizen of one day often found himself doomed upon the next, and many happy homes were, without a moment's warning, broken up, and the father or mother, and sometimes both, hurried off to prison and the mockery of a trial. The delusion finally furnished the cause of its downfall. The Rev. Jeremiah Shepherd of Lynn was denounced as a wizard. The charge was so manifestly absurd, and the friends of the worthy pastor made such demonstrations of opposition, that the judges called a halt. The excitement cooled as quickly as it had risen. Those confined in jail were released, and in many cases compensated for lost time; and most of the girls whose antics had caused the mischief, came before the church, humbly confessed their errors—the blame for which was duly laid upon Satan, who had possessed them—and pleaded for forgiveness. Thus ended this most weird and bloody chapter in the history of our city and vicinity. It reads little like a story of real life actually lived near the spot we call home; yet such it is. The superstitions of those old days are gone — or exchanged; but whether exchanged or gone will not be told until two more centuries have passed by. Perhaps, then, some poet will sing of the romance of these days as sweetly as Whittier has sung the requiem of the days gone by :

> " How has New England's romance fled,
>> Even as a vision of the morning!
> Its rites foredone,—its guardians dead,—
> Its priestesses, bereft of dread,
>> Waking the veriest urchin's scorning!
> Gone like the Indian wizard's yell,
>> And fire-dance round the magic rock!
> Forgotten like the Druid's spell
>> At moonrise by his holy oak!
> No more along the shadowy glen
> Glide the dim ghosts of murdered men;
> No more the unquiet churchyard dead
> Glimpse upward from their turfy bed,
>> Startling the traveller, late and lone;
> As on some night of starless weather
> They silently commune together,
>> Each sitting on his own headstone!
> The roofless house, decayed, deserted,
> Its living tenants all departed,
> No longer rings with midnight revel
> Of witch, or ghost, or goblin evil;
> No pale blue flame sends out its flashes
> Through creviced roof or shattered sashes!—
> The witch-grass round the hazel spring
> May sharply to the night-air sing,
> But there no more shall withered hags
> Refresh at ease their broomstick nags,
> Or taste those hazel-shadowed waters
> As beverage meet for Satan's daughters;
> No more their mimic tones be heard,—
> The mew of cat,—the chirp of bird,—
> Shrill blending with the hoarser laughter
> Of the fell demon following after!"

Moll Pitcher.

"SHE stood upon a bare, tall crag
    Which overlooked her rugged cot —
    A wasted, gray and meagre hag,
    In features evil as her lot.
She had the crooked nose of a witch,
    And a crooked back and chin;
And in her gait she had a hitch,
And in her hand she carried a switch
    To aid her work of sin —
A twig of wizard hazel, which
Had grown beside a haunted ditch."

Whittier must have given his then youthful fancy loose rein in this word-picture of our famous townswoman. Doubtless he described what, according to the popular fancy, a witch should resemble. But Moll Pitcher was no witch, though doubtless if she had lived in the days of the witchcraft frenzy, she would have been hanged as such with little ceremony. But it was less than three-quarters of a century ago that she lived in her little cottage, opposite the head of Pearl street, on the north side of Essex, where for fifty years she solved the doubts and mysteries which troubled her contemporaries. Her father, Capt. John Dimond, commanded a small vessel sailing out of Marblehead. She was born in 1738, and early married Robert Pitcher, a Lynn shoemaker — a man of no force of character — and the chief burden of the support of the little family, one son and three daughters, early fell on her. Her ancestors had borne a reputation as wizards of greater or less attainment, a favorite accomplishment of her grandfather having been to pace up and down among the graves in the church-yard during the most furious storms, and direct the course of vessels attempting to make the harbor, his voice plainly audible to the sailors, no matter how loudly the storm might roar, or how far out the vessel might be. With such a reputation ready-made in the family, it is, perhaps, little wonder that young Mistress Pitcher sought to lighten the pressure of poverty by the exercise of her inherited gifts. But whatever was the motive that first impelled her to practice the art of

soothsaying, her early success was great, and her fame spread until her musical
name became a household word not only throughout this land and England, but
in every port where the Yankee sailor spun his yarns, were related stories of the
Lynn pythoness, which doubtless suffered no loss of embellishment or detail
because of the inborn credulity of the sailor boys. Her powers lay in no special
direction, but she was sought alike by the swain in doubt as to the feelings of
his fair one; by the maiden anxious to know of the safety of her sailor lover;
by the sailor, to know if he should have a safe return; by the merchant, solicitous of the success of his ventures; and by the noble, to learn the future course
of the affairs of state. The well-worn path to her cottage was trodden by rich
and poor, high and low, alike. No matter what their station in the outside
world, within the brown cottage beneath the shadow of High Rock, in the presence of the renowned fortune-teller, they stood on a common level, and for a
consideration could learn the whereabouts of lost property or friends, or get the
merest peep behind the curtain of the future.

Lewis, who was familiar with her appearance, having known her, leaves a
picture very different from the fancy sketch of the Quaker bard: " She was of
medium height and size for a woman, with a good form and agreeable manners.
Her head, phrenologically considered, was somewhat capacious, her forehead
broad and full, her hair dark brown, her nose inclining to be long, and her face
pale and thin. Her countenance was intellectual, and she had the contour of
face and expression which, without being positively beautiful, is nevertheless

Mary Pitcher

decidedly interesting,—a thoughtful, pensive, sometimes downcast look, almost
approaching to melancholy,—an eye, when she looked at you, of calm and keen
penetration,—and an expression of intelligent discernment half mingled with a
glance of shrewdness."

What was the secret of the remarkable power of Moll Pitcher? Here she dwelt all the years of a long life, going in and out before the people, her life open before them; reputable, charitable, and given to no occult or mysterious rites other than scanning the bottom of a tea-cup or musing over the cards, and it is most likely that she had little regard for these ceremonies, but used them to gain time while cautiously watching her visitors for a clue to their history or desires; but more often she calmly looked her customers over and talked with them face to face. Yet her fame increased with her years. The stories that are told of her achievements, not only in piercing the secrets of the future, but in solving the mysteries of the current happenings, would rouse the smile of incredulity were they not recorded by persons of undoubted veracity and reliability. Possibly to great native shrewdness and tact in divining the hidden thoughts and desires of her visitors was added in a high degree the clairvoyant faculty; but probably most of her revelations could be accounted for without resort to this intangible quality. According to the proverb, " it is the unexpected that happens;" not that the occurrences of every day are not the natural outcome of antecedent acts, but because men, in forming their expectations, ordinarily think along the line of their desires, rather than according to the logic of the events of their past lives. If, therefore, the sibyl, having gained from the unsuspecting guest the main facts of his life to the time of their meeting, has the logical force to deduce from them their natural outcome in his after years, the " fortune" which she may tell him will very likely be vastly different from his anticipations, but will probably be the things which must inevitably result from his course of life. To a mind on the alert and trained by long experience, the slightest admission may be a sufficient clew to the secret of a life. Doubtless Moll Pitcher made a great many mistakes. These would be little heard of and soon forgotten, but a prediction verified under extraordinary circumstances was sure to be talked of as a wonder, and to lose nothing in each repetition; and among the thousands who sought her counsel, there could hardly fail of being many who would unconsciously furnish her with the data for a wonderfully accurate "fortune." But even this supposition will not satisfactorily account for many of her achievements in her peculiar line, and it is easier to lay

MOLL PITCHER'S COTTAGE.

the secret of them at the door of clairvoyance than to trace them to their actual origin. Whatever was the secret of her power, she was the most successful fortune-teller of her day; she had no equals among her predecessors, and since she died there has been none like her. The home she lived in still stands near its old foundation, on Essex, at the head of Pearl street. If only its walls could be induced to tell the many strange things they have heard in their day, and the names of all the persons who crossed the sibyl's palm with the magic key to her knowledge of the future, what a wondrously interesting story could be written! She was married on the 2nd of October, 1760, and died April 9th, 1813.

> "Even she, our own weird heroine,
> Sole Pythoness of ancient Lynn,
>   Sleeps calmly where the living laid her;
> And the wide realm of sorcery,
> Left by its latest mistress free,
>   Hath found no gray and skilled invader."

The Sea Serpent.

THIS strange wanderer of the seas can scarcely be classed as an exclusively Lynn institution, but in the early part of the present century he created a tremendous sensation here and hereabouts. That there was such a visitor to our shores and bay in the early summer of 1819 and several seasons after, is true past question; it was through attempts to describe him, and worse still, to estimate his length, that many reputations well established as to truth and veracity received a wrench from which they have never recovered. When Col. T. H. Perkins, a well-known resident of Boston, was asked by an English friend whether he had heard of the sea serpent, he replied: "Unfortunately I have seen it." He felt that a shadow had somehow closed in upon him from which he was unable to emerge.

His snakeship's comings were as unannounced as his departures were unceremonious, and he was frequently seen taking his morning swim along the shores, his head elevated at a good sight-seeing distance above the waves. Whether the people he saw were too inquisitive, or the country not to his liking, is not known, but he declined to fix his residence here, though no doubt he could have made very advantageous terms as a permanent summer attraction. A recently published letter by a fellow townsman gives as good a description of him as any we have seen.

"LYNN, MASS., June 26, 1881.

MR. C. F. HOLDER.

Dear Sir:—Yours of the 24th inst. came duly to hand, and, in reply to that part of it relating to the account given by myself of a strange fish, serpent, or some other marine animal called a sea serpent, I have to say that I saw him on a pleasant, calm summer morning of August, 1819, from Long Beach, Lynn, now Nahant. At this time he was about a quarter of a mile away; but the water was so smooth that I could plainly see his head and the motion of his body, but not distinctly enough to give a good description of him. Later in the day I saw him again off 'Red Rock.' He then passed along about one hundred feet from where I stood, with head about two feet out of the water, and his speed was about the ordinary of a common steamer. What I saw of his length was from fifty to sixty feet.

It was very difficult to count the bunches or humps (not fins) upon his back, as, by the undulating motion, they did not all appear at once. This accounts, in part, for the varied descriptions given of him by different parties. His appearance upon the surface of the water was occasional and but for a short time. The color of his skin was dark, differing but little from the water, or the back of any common fish. This is the best description I can give of him from my own observation, and I saw the monster just as truly, although not quite so clearly, as I ever saw anything.

This matter has been treated by many as a hoax, fish story, or a seaside phenomenon to bring trade and profit to the watering-places; but, notwithstanding all this, there is no doubt in my mind that some kind of an uncommon or strange rover in the form of a snake or a serpent, called an ichthyosaurus, plesiosaurus, or some other long-named marine animal, has been seen by hundreds of men and boys in our own, if not in other waters. And five persons beside myself — Amos Lawrence, Samuel Cabot and James Prince, of Boston, Benjamin F. Newhall, of Saugus, and John Marston, of Swampscott — bore public testimony of having seen him at the time.

Yours Truly,

NATHAN D. CHASE."

The gentlemen named were all interviewed at the time, and their testimony, to make it, if possible, more conclusive, was sworn to before a magistrate, and differed only in detail from that of Mr. Chase, except that Mr. Marston thought he might have been a hundred feet long. At various times and in various places, from Nahant to Nova Scotia, his serpentine majesty has suddenly raised his head above the waves, carrying wonder and affright to the hearts of all beholders. All tell about the same story of him with the exception of the crew of the bark "Pauline," of London. Their testimony, taken before a magistrate at Liverpool, was:

"Borough of Liverpool, in the County Palatine of Lancaster, to wit: We, the undersigned, captain, officers and crew of the bark Pauline of

Liverpool, in the County of Lancaster, in the United Kingdom of Great Britain and Ireland, do solemnly and sincerely declare that on July 8th, 1875, in latitute 5 deg. S. and longitude 35 deg. W., we observed three large sperm whales, and one of them was gripped round the body with two turns of what appeared to be a huge serpent. The head and tail appeared to have a length beyond the coils of about thirty feet, and its girth eight or nine feet. The serpent whirled its victim round and round for about fifteen minutes, and then suddenly dragged the whale to the bottom head first. George Drevar, *Master;* Horatio Thompson, John Henderson Landells, Owen Baker, William Lewarn."

That was quite a fish story, but it by no means measured their capacity in that line, for five days later three of the same ship's crew made affidavit that they had seen the serpent, his head "elevated some sixty feet in the air." What length of body and tail would be required to enable the serpent to elevate his head sixty feet in the air, we leave for others to figure out; but it seems a pity that they could not have been contented to let a good enough story alone. At intervals during these later years this strange wanderer of the seas has put in an appearance now here, now there; but those across whose path he has swum have become very guarded in their references to him, owing, possibly, to sundry unkind references to the unaqueous condition of their ship stores. But the local descriptions given of this king of the serpents have attracted wide attention in scientific circles, and even inspired one poet's muse:

"Welter upon the waters, mighty one,
    And stretch thee in the ocean's trough of brine;
Turn thy wet scales up to the wind and sun,
    And toss the billows from thy flashing fin;
    Heave thy deep breathings to the ocean's din,
And bound upon its ridges in thy pride;
    Or dive down to its lowest depths, and in
The caverns where its unknown monsters hide,
Measure thy length beneath the gulf stream tide;
    Or rest thee on the navel of that sea
Where, floating on the maelstrom, abide
    The Krakens, sheltering under Norway's lee—
But go not to Nahant, lest men should swear
You are a great deal bigger than you are."

— J. G. BRAINERD.

NAHANT BREAKERS.

City of Lynn.

N the fourteenth day of May, 1850, the town organization, under which Lynn had lived peacefully and happily for two centuries, was superseded by the city form of government. The change was not made without a struggle, and for two successive years Mr. George Hood, one of the most public-spirited men of the time, successfully led the opposition to the proposed measure; but the majority of the people were against him. Notwithstanding his pronounced opposition, his fellow-citizens were quick to see that his course was governed by motives of public spirit and solicitous regard for the best welfare of the town, and at the first election of city officers, he was chosen Mayor by a small majority. The first City Government was organized on the date above named, with Daniel C. Baker as President of the Council, and Richard Bassett as City Clerk. Under the careful guidance of Mayor Hood, the machinery of the new city was soon made to run smoothly. His large business experience and knowledge of public affairs, gained by several years' service in the General Court and other public positions, specially fitted him for the duties of Mayor, and he devoted himself with as much energy to promoting the interests of the city as he had to opposing the acceptance of the city charter. The second year he was re-elected by a very large majority, showing that the people recognized his faithful service in their behalf. The third year he declined a renomination. Among the more important events of the two years of Mayor Hood's administration may be mentioned the readjustment of the hours of labor, whereby ten hours came to be accepted as a day's work — in bringing this change about, Mayor Hood bore a leading part — the High School building on High street was dedicated; an effort was made to preserve Long Beach from the encroachments of the sea by planting a line of red cedars along the ridge; the excavation in Dungeon Rock was begun by Hiram Marble; a grand reception was tendered to Louis Kossuth; and the sewing machine was introduced. The shoe industry was in a highly prosperous condition. Largely through the efforts of Mr. Samuel Brimblecom, who died in 1850, the methods of carrying on the business had been simplified and systematized, and the manufacturers found a ready market for their product at remunerative prices. The total valuation of the city was $4,834,843, and the municipality started out with a debt of $56,960.

In 1852 Swampscott was set off as a separate town, and the following year Nahant gained her majority. The following years were uneventful beyond the ordinary happenings of New England towns. The financial depression of 1857 rested heavily upon rich and poor alike, and during the struggle to regain the ground lost, the foundation was laid for the great strike of 1860, which created a decided sensation throughout the country. The hanging of John Brown, in 1859, again roused the slavery-hating citizens of Lynn to a high pitch of indignation, and the bells were tolled at sunrise, noon and sunset. In 1860 the valuation of the city was $9,649,065, population 19,087, showing a gain of 50 per cent. in population, and 100 per cent. in wealth, during the decade.

In 1861 came the news of the fall of Fort Sumter. The first call for troops by President Lincoln met with a prompt response from Lynn. In five hours after the proclamation was received, two full companies were armed and ready for duty, and the following terse dispatch was sent to headquarters: "We have more men than guns—what shall we do?" At eleven o'clock the next day, April 16th, they left for the seat of war. These two companies — the Lynn Light Infantry, Capt. George T. Newhall, and the Lynn City Guards, Capt. James Hudson, Jr.—were attached to the Eighth Massachusetts Regiment, of which Timothy Munroe, of Lynn, was colonel. Capt. Newhall is still among us, hale and hearty, and wields a pen as mighty

HON. GEORGE HOOD.

for peace, morality and earnest living as his sword was for freedom and the integrity of the Union. The regiment performed honorable, though not very bloody service, and returned after its three months' term without the loss, by death, of a man. Meanwhile the war spirit had kept at fever heat, and enlistments went rapidly forward. Throughout the war Lynn supported the Government loyally, and gave of her men and means without stint. Large and enthusiastic war meetings were held, and great inducements in the way of bounties for volunteers offered, with the result of keeping her quota more than full. During the war Lynn furnished 3,274 men for the field — 230 more than her full quota. Many of those who went into the war from Lynn in private or sub-ordinate positions rose to places of honor and distinction, and not a few who went came not back. Out of those who did return has been organized the largest Post of the Grand Army of the Republic in the country. Those were stirring times in Lynn, and to describe the great war meetings, the departure of troops for the front, the rejoicings over victories achieved, the funeral honors paid to slain soldiers, and the other moving incidents of those memorable days, would require larger limits than this volume affords.

Hon. Peter M. Neal was Mayor of the city during 1862–5. In those times the duties devolving upon the chief magistrates of our cities were varied and constant. In addition to the routine work of the office, there were the added duties arising from the raising and equipping of troops, the general oversight of all relief operations, and the many questions and requests coming from the friends of those at the front. During the four years of his administration, he generally worked from sixteen to eighteen hours a day. He was indefatigable in his exertions in alleviating the suffer-
ings of our soldiers and their families,
and many times visited the army and
hospitals, carrying good cheer and
messages from home to those in the
field, and relief and comfort to the
wounded. After the close of the
war, for many years he continued
his care and service for the soldiers
and their families, obtaining for
many pensions from the Government, although he would never take
any compensation for his efforts.
Mr. Neal is a native of Maine, and
was born in North Berwick Sept.
21, 1811. His parents were Quakers, and he received his education
and early training in the Friends'
schools. After leaving school, until
1850 he was engaged in teaching in
Maine. In that year he came to
Lynn and engaged in the lumber
business, in which he still continues.

HON. PETER M. NEAL.

The burning of the old City Hall, which from the time of its building, in 1814, until 1832 had stood in the center of the Common, and thereafter on South Common street, left the city without an official home until the new City Hall was completed in 1867. The new building was dedicated on Saturday, Nov. 30. The whole day was generally observed as a holiday. The dedicatory exercises were of a very interesting nature, consisting of addresses, poem, etc., and, what was of equal interest to very many, a free collation in the basement, served at noon. The beautiful structure thus dedicated is justly regarded as one of the chief ornaments of the city. The many conveniences for the transaction of public business which it affords, and the beneficent influence which it has exerted upon the architecture of the city, have made it worth the cost, which was about $312,000. From this time on, the growth and development of the city has been rapid. The shoe industry, which from the earliest times had been carried on in the little shops scattered here and there over the city, had been gradually developing toward the factory system, and to center about the railroad station. There were no steam engines in Lynn at that time, but the change taking place in the methods of the business rendered them a necessity, and they were soon after introduced; and during the few years ending in 1874 many of

LYNN CITY HALL.

the large factories were built. Business was good, real estate rapidly advanced in price, and values of all kinds rapidly expanded. The following year the financial crash came. Real estate declined more rapidly than it had risen, failures were numerous, and business had a blue time generally. This depression lasted nearly two years. The recovery was gradual but healthy, and since that time the growth of the city, while being measurably rapid, has been regulated by the demand of the time rather than by any speculative movement. The shoe business and its collateral branches has steadily expanded. The later years have been prolific of labor troubles, and the inducements held out by various country towns have caused many of our manufacturers to locate a part of their business outside the city, where they hoped to be free from disturbance of this nature. At present, many towns in Maine and New Hampshire receive their principal business impulse from the operations of Lynn capital and brains in their midst, and hence may almost be looked upon as outlying wards of the city proper.

The two hundred and fiftieth anniversary of the settlement of Lynn was celebrated in 1879, on the 17th of June. In all these many years she has enjoyed a steady increase both in population and business importance. Though possessing a large water frontage, the harbor is approachable only by a small class of vessels, the channel being both narrow and shallow. Yet when the Lynn yachtsmen come together in their annual regattas, the harbor presents an animated appearance. In respect to her harbor she has

been, for all commercial purposes, less fortunately situated than some of her sisters who started in life about the same time with herself. Yet this very fact is now seen to have contributed largely to her success. Little of her capital and few of her citizens being engaged in shipping or foreign commerce, the embargoes and blockades resulting from our numerous wars inflicted very little loss or hardship here, and she was left free to develope the peculiar industry for which her people and soil seem best adapted; and having a home market for her manufacture, the disturbances at home and abroad, which oftentimes had a well-nigh disastrous effect upon many seaboard towns, troubled her but little, and that only incidentally. The foundations of the city's prosperity were laid broad and deep, and consist not more in the reputation for excellence, finish and cheapness of her product, than upon the inborn enterprise and ability of her manufacturers and the skill and faithful work of her mechanics. And enough business has gone from Lynn, to escape labor troubles and take advantage of the inducements offered by country towns, to make, if all were collected together, another city of almost equal size and importance with herself.

The census of 1885 credits Lynn with a population of 45,867, with 13,278 polls, a valuation of $28,459,243, and a tax roll of $533,130.53; 7,144 houses

on 564 streets, places and courts, make up the city.   A Police Department
with 44 patrolmen guard the peace of the town; a Fire Department of five
steamers, one chemical engine, four hose companies, and two hook and
ladder companies, protect us from conflagrations.   One High, seven Grammar
and sixty-four Primary schools, besides numerous private schools, provide for
the education of our youth, and the spires of twenty-six churches point the
way to a better life.   A free public library of 32,000 volumes furnishes good
reading to whomsoever chooses to avail themselves of its advantages, and the
social, charitable and protective associations number one hundred and three.
Connection with the outer world is maintained by the Boston & Maine, Boston,
Revere Beach and Lynn, and the Lynn and Boston (Horse) Railroad Companies.   Five National Banks facilitate our business exchanges, and two Savings
Banks guard the small savings of the people.   It may, therefore, be asserted that
Lynn is not only a city having a history and a goodly heritage, but also is possessed of all the advantages and appliances of a live, modern manufacturing
town, and an industry that is destined in the future, as it has done in the past,
to keep her in the front rank of the sisterhood of the cities in the Commonwealth.   As we pass on, we shall have occasion to examine many features of
our modern city more in detail, and to get something of an idea of her resources
and developments of her social life.

BREAKWATER. LYNN. CHRISTMAS 1885.

MT. VERNON STREET.

Leading Industries.

THE beginnings of shoemaking in Lynn were exceedingly small — "like a grain of mustard seed, which indeed is the least of all seeds, but when it is grown, is the greatest among herbs." In like manner has the shoe industry grown, until our goodly city, with many sister communities in the Commonwealth, and New England as well, finds shelter "in the branches thereof." Probably Philip Kertland, the first Lynn shoemaker, did not lay claim to more than ordinary skill in the art, and for many years those who followed in his footsteps were content to do as he had done. The best shoes worn by the Lynn dames came from England and France. Those constructed here were made of neat's leather, and were serviceable, if not handsome. The sole leather was worked with the flesh side out, and for nearly two centuries both shoes were made on the same last. About the year 1670 shoes began to be cut with broad straps for buckles, which were worn by women as well as men. Fifty years later buckles for ladies' shoes went out of fashion. The coming of John Adam Dagyr in 1750 gave the trade of shoemaking in Lynn the turn and impetus which led to its adoption as the leading industry of the place. He was a thorough workman, and produced shoes equal to the best made in England. The Lynn craftsmen were apt scholars, and it was not long before the fame of the Lynn shoe had spread throughout the colonies. The little, square shoemaker's shop became an institution, and fathers and sons in their spare hours, particularly in winter, worked alongside the journeymen and apprentices, the number working in a single shop ranging from four to eight. In the years

preceding the introduction of machinery these shoe shops had become very numerous. The shoes were cut at the establishments of the bosses, and given out to be made through the town. The uppers were called " shoes," and the soles " stuffs," and thread, wax and everything necessary to make the shoe were

PRIMITIVE SHOEMAKING.

supplied by the bosses with the shoes. The ladies of the household had quite as important a part in the work as the men. They stitched, or bound, the uppers while the men were preparing the soles. The sewing-machine made quick despatch with the time-honored occupation of our mothers and grand-mothers, but Lucy Larcom has immortalized their work in her pathetic poem of Hannah Binding Shoes. The invention, or rather the perfecting, of the McKay

"Spring and winter, Hannah's at the window binding shoes."

machine in 1862 put an end to the old-style methods of shoemaking, and the modest shoe shops which were scattered all over the town were gradually turned over to the uses of the pigs and chickens, and the shoe factory became an insti-tution. These naturally clustered as closely as possible about the railroad. Mr. John Wooldredge was one of the first to see the advantages of the labor-saving machines, and it was he who, in 1852, brought the first sewing-machines to Lynn, and ten years later, first applied steam power to the manufacture of shoes. It was not till the close of the war, in 1865, that the use of steam engines in shoe factories became general. With machinery came the minute sub-divisions of the labor of making the shoe, so that, in place of the three, and possibly four, persons who would once have performed the labor upon a shoe, the work is now shared by not less than thirty-four.

No more interesting trip can be taken, than with a competent guide, to go through one of the large shoe factories and watch the processes by which abstract particles of leather, iron, cloth, buttons and other things, in all more than one hundred in number, gradually come together in the form of a shoe.   Commencing at the basement, one finds himself in a most confusing medley of brawny men in scant clothing, for it is hot down there at all seasons, huge machines which run with a clatter and thud that suggest great power, and piles of leather in all stages of manufacture, from the whole side to the soles which have been sorted, sized and tied up ready for the making rooms above.   In this room we find the stripper, sole cutter, sorter and tier-up : and one cannot help wondering if those who are running the stripping and dinking machines are as indifferent to the loss of a finger or possibly a hand as they seem to be.   We are next shown into the cutting room where the upper leather and linings are prepared.   There is nothing exciting here.   These twenty or more gentlemen who are ranged around the room, each at his cutting-board, work with a deliberation and care which is seen in no other part of the factory, but necessary to faithful work.   In this room we find four more divisions of the work — 1, outside cutter ; 2, lining cutter ; 3, trimming cutter ; 4, dier-out.   Following our guide we mount another flight of steps and find ourselves in the stitching room.   The energetic clatter of the different busy machines render us oblivious to the conductor's explanatory remarks, and we content ourselves with watching the continued evolution of the shoe under the busy, skilful fingers of the operatives.   The uppers pass first into the hands of the lining maker, then to the closer, third, seam-rubber ; fourth, back-stayer ; fifth, front-stayer ; sixth, closer-on ; seventh, turner ; eighth, top-stitcher ; ninth, button-hole cutter ; tenth, corder ; eleventh, button-sewer. On casting up our account so far, we find that twenty persons have had a part in making our shoe.   From the stitching room we are taken to the finishing room, where the bottoms and uppers, which have thus far been travelling by different routes are finally brought together.   In this room, as in the stitching room and basement, everything is lively.   Men and boys are working as if for life and scarcely stop to bestow a look upon the visiting party.   Racks and horses filled with shoes in all stages of completion fill the floor, and numerous odd looking machines are located at convenient spots.   At one end of this room the component parts of the shoe come together in the hands of the stock-fitter, whom we number twenty-one in our list, and are passed from hand to hand until they arrive at the other end completed, ready for packing and shipment.   From the stock-fitter we watch our shoe go into the hands of the laster, who, with a dozen of his fellows, works at an odd-shaped bench.   Attention is attracted to one who is evidently a veteran.   Taking a preparatory chew of tobacco, which he carefully stows away in one cheek, and with a backward toss of the head filling the other with something less than a gill of sharp tacks, he proceeds to last our shoe : and with caring for the tobacco, working the tacks one by one to his lips with his tongue, and dropping an occasional emphatic ejaculation as he drops a tack or pounds his thumb, his mouth is kept as busy as his hands.   The cutting and lasting departments of the shoe factory are the only ones which have not been successfully invaded by the labor-saving machines, and these are about the most important in the factory.   Upon the good judgment and close calculation of the cutter depend, in large measure, uniformity in the quality of the product and the profits of the business, for no degree of ability or foresight in the management can counteract the ravages of a wasteful cutter ;

WILLOW STREET, LOOKING TOWARD CENTRAL SQUARE.

and upon the faithfulness and skill of the laster depend the fit and set of the shoe, assuming, of course, that the work leading up to the laster has been faithfully done. Hence it is, that good lasters are always in demand, and their Union has maintained a more independent position than any other organization connected with the craft has been able to assume. Invention has now turned its attention to this department, and a young Lynn mechanic has produced a lasting machine which promises to be successful, though it has not yet come into general use. From the laster the shoe goes to the sole-layer, whom we number 23; next to the McKay stitcher, 24; and then on to the beater-out, 25; trimmer, 26; edge-setter, 27; liner, 28; nailer, who fastens on the heel, 29; shaver, 30; buffer, 31; burnisher, 32; channeller, 33; and the shoe which started as a number of abstract particles so little time ago, is now completed ready to be stamped and placed in neat paper cartons by the packer, and shipped to its destination. In our enumeration we have named only those who perform the most important parts in the making of a shoe. But in the different processes of tanning the leather and numerous subordinate parts in the shoe factory, the united labor of more than fifty people are required to produce a modern pair of ladies' shoes.

The shoe and leather industry is found clustered as closely as possible about the railroad, and in the "shoe district;" the most of the buildings which are not occupied as manufactories of shoes or leather are devoted either to some branch of business intimately associated therewith, or to the dispensing of animal comforts. This district lies almost wholly between Liberty and Market streets, and Broad, Silsbee and Mulberry streets. Some of the finest factories in the city are on Willow street. Looking down the street toward Central square at any hour of the day, one gets a vivid impression of the busy life that constantly throbs through this street and the great artery beyond. On the right are the buildings occupied by the Lynn Shoe Supply Co. and T. J. Little & Co.; on the left the factories of Keene Brothers, A. M. & J. H. Preble, W. A. Dole & Whittredge, and M. J. Worthley and the leather firm of Lothrop & Bowen. Passing Oxford street, on the left are seen the large Tebbetts factory and the fine Mower building. Included in this sec-
tion is the large building
occupied by Morgan &
Dore, on Oxford street,
shown on page seventy-
nine. This enterprising
firm do only a portion of
their business in Lynn,
having large factories at
Pittsfield, N.H., and Rich-
mond, Me. Keene Bros.
also do a large business at
Skowhegan, Me. Passing
into Central square, we
get an animated view of

CHAS. D. PECKER & CO.'S FACTORY.

that busy center. On the right is the large Fuller block, occupied by

Charles D. Pecker & Co., who also have a large factory at Great Falls, N. H., and by numerous express and other offices. Many of the buildings on the square are scarcely appropriate to the place they occupy, but in the march of progress they will doubtless ere long be replaced by more comely structures. Mt. Vernon street is occupied by some of our most enterprising firms. The sign of L. S. Johnson on the corner, and the name of F. W. Breed, have come to be regarded as landmarks, and the whole street has a substantial and prosperous appearance. Exchange street, the Pine street of the olden time, is a busy spot, but the buildings are mostly small and of wood. Union street, from the square to Broad street, has, during the past few years, taken rapid strides forward, and now some of our strongest firms and best equipped factories are located here. The Brown and Ingalls buildings, on the left, were the first brick factories on the street. The Ashcroft building, on the corner of Washington and Union streets, is a substantial and comely structure, and some live firms are located in it. The firm of Shepherd, Murphy & Co., who occupy the corner store, are among our most enterprising young concerns, who do a safe and constantly increasing business. The

CENTRAL SQUARE.

firm of John S. Bartlett & Co. occupy the large building on the opposite corner, successors of the name and fame of the old firm of B. F. Doak & Co. The new Buffum block, opposite Washington street, is a handsome structure, and a decided ornament to that section. The factory of Mr. J. N. Smith was one of the first large buildings built in this section, and is one of the few large wooden factories now remaining. The large Alley building, near the foot of the street, is a very convenient, well-equipped block, and is occupied by Kimball Brothers, who also have a large factory in Gardiner, Me., and the firm of Charles Buffum & Co., a substantial firm of long standing. Mr. Buffum antedates most of the shoe manufacturers in Lynn now in active business. Broad street was at one time headquarters for much of the business done in the town, but its glory has in a measure departed. The handsome factory of V. K. & A. H. Jones, on the corner of Beach street, and the large block at the head of Buffum's wharf, are the only large factories on this street. The lower end of Market street has always been identified with the shoe and leather industry. In the cut previously shown of this thoroughfare in 1820 are numerous tanneries and shoe shops. The Lennox block on the right, and the Lancaster and the Martin buildings on the left, are substantial and commodious structures. The large blocks of factories on either side of the street above the railroad, erected many years since by Hon. Samuel M. Bubier, contribute a fixed, settled aspect to that section which is lacking in some parts of the city. Mr. Bubier has been identified with the shoe business in Lynn for a long time. He was formerly an extensive manufacturer, and has witnessed all the changes which have taken place. He has now retired from that branch of the business, and devotes himself to the care of his large property and to supplying power to many buildings in the vicinity of

THE ASHCROFT BUILDING, UNION STREET.

Market street, besides his own. He has always taken an active interest in the affairs of the town, and served one term as mayor in 1877. Munroe street has several large factories, notably that of P. P. Sherry, which at the time of its erection was the highest building in the city. Mr. Sherry laid down the principle, which has since been extensively followed, that land grows cheaper the higher up you go ; but considerations quite as potent as that named are the good light and freedom from dust afforded by the upper rooms in high buildings, which is essential to good workmanship, particularly in the finishing rooms. On Oxford street is the handsome new building of D. A. Caldwell & Co., occupied by D. A. Caldwell & Co. and J. F. Swain & Co., erected in 1885. This is one of the best appointed factories in the city, and in the design of the front elevation, more attention was paid to architectural effect than has been done in the plans of many of our large factories. The other large establishments on Oxford street are those of C. S. Sweetser and Aaron F. Smith, and the handsome new building erected on the site of C. A. Coffin's factory, burned in 1885.

Passing out Washington street we come to the large block, recently completed, of Valpey & Anthony, one of the finest in the city. The course of our wanderings has brought us nearly back to the point of starting, and during our walk we have inspected the principal part of the shoe district.

The list of shoe manufacturers in Lynn number one hundred and seventy-six, ranging from single individuals manufacturing in a small way to large corporations and firms running several large factories and employing hundreds of hands. Nearly all grades of women's shoes and slippers are made, from the cheapest slipper to the finest French kid boot.

THE ALLEY BUILDING, UNION STREET.

The methods of transacting the shoe business have changed quite as much as the processes of manufacturing. At first a home market was found for most of the product. Then, after the coming of Dagyr and the improvements in the workmanship and quality of the goods which he introduced, the surplus found a market in Boston, being transported

V. K. & A. H. JONES' FACTORY, BROAD STREET.

thither in bags, boxes, or in any convenient package, sometimes on the backs of the bosses, who walked to Boston and returned in the same manner, but more commonly by team. After the close of the War of the Revolution, the business became very much depressed, owing to the competition of shoes made abroad. The matter was brought to the attention of Congress, then in session in Philadelphia, through the efforts of Ebenezer Breed, of Lynn, and Stephen Collins, a native of Lynn, but doing business in Philadelphia ; and a tariff was placed upon foreign shoes, which had the immediate effect of reviving the industry. Thus the shoe manufacturing industry was the first to be taken under the protecting wing of the Government. Mr. Breed subsequently introduced into the city the manufacture of morocco leather, for which he received a vote of thanks from the National Committee of Manufactures and Commerce. He also secured the establishment of the Lynn Post-Office in 1793. For many years he did a very large business, but late in life misfortune overtook him, and he ended his days in the almshouse. Much of the manufacturing sixty years ago was done by Micajah C. Pratt, James Pratt, Nathan Breed, Isaiah Breed and Nathan D. Chase, whose manufactories were all on Broad street. Isaiah Breed's office was in his dwelling-house on what is now the corner of Broad and Exchange streets. For many years they received very little money for their goods, but took their pay in barter, and in turn paid their workmen in orders on store-keepers in Lynn and Salem. This system kept the workmen always poor and in debt, and in 1842 they rebelled against it, and have since received their pay in cash.

THE NEW BUFFUM BLOCK, UNION STREET.

From Boston the shoes were sent South, and for many years were sold at auction, oftentimes being sent thither by cargoes, the first full cargo being sent in 1818. Between 1820 and 1829 this was abandoned and the jobbers from the southern states came hither to purchase, that they might be able the better to select goods suitable for their localities. This custom is still kept up to a degree, but twice each year the large manufacturers send their salesmen west and south, who bring their samples to the attention of every dealer whose custom is worth having. These salesmen are, with rare exceptions, young men of character and proved capacity, who do credit to the industry which they

FACTORY OF C. H. ABORN & CO. AND C. W. VARNEY & CO., BROAD STREET.

represent. If there be any modern tendency in the trade toward a change, it is to be found in the disposition of many of the large houses to sell directly to retailers without the intervention of middle-men, and there are those who predict that this system will be the outcome of the present degree of competition among manufacturers.

Tanning became an industry in Lynn some years before shoemaking was introduced. Francis Ingalls, who came hither with his brother Edmund, chose for his habitation the pleasant slope which leads down to Swampscott beach, and on Humphrey street, by the brook, built his tannery, and Alonzo Lewis states that he saw the remains of the vats used in curing the leather. The business was continued for many years with varying success, at times highly prosperous, and at times leather could be bought in other markets cheaper than it could be manufactured here ; but in these last years the bulk of the business has centered about Salem and Peabody. In 1800, through the efforts of Eben-ezer Breed, the manufacture of mo-rocco leather was introduced. The first factory was established by Wil-liam Rose on the south side of the

THE LENNOX BLOCK, MARKET STREET.

Common, opposite where the fountain now is. This industry has grown with the town, and now is only second in importance to the manufacture of shoes. The manufactories are not confined to any particular section of the city. The mammoth establishment of A. B. Martin & Co. on Market street, and of Henry A. Pevear & Sons near Boston street, are among the largest in town. Several

D. A. CALDWELL & CO.'S FACTORY, OXFORD STREET.

large concerns are located in Harrison court, others on Munroe, Broad and Beach streets. The large factory of Lu-cius Beebe & Sons, on Western avenue, is one of the most complete establish-ments of its kind in the East. There are twenty-seven firms engaged in this branch of manufacture, and the product finds a market in nearly every shoe town in the country. In addition to the two leading branches of the shoe and leather industry already mentioned, there are many others directly contributory to them. Among them may be mentioned fifty-seven dealers and manufacturers of boot and shoe soles, heels, stiffenings, &c., sixty-six stitching-rooms, twenty dealers and manufacturers of findings and supplies, thirteen manufacturers of boot and shoe machinery, besides numerous other sub-divisions of the business. In the production of labor-saving machinery Lynn mechanics have made several notable contributions, which are to be seen in every well-regulated shoe factory. One of the latest inventions, and one which promises to

MORGAN & DORE'S FACTORY, OXFORD STREET.

become of great practical utility, is a lasting machine which lasts a shoe perfectly

LUCIUS BEEBE & SONS' FACTORY, WEST LYNN.

EARLY MORNING VIEW ON UNION STREET.

in the time a shoemaker of fifty years ago would be getting his tools together. Another industry inseperably allied to the manufacture of shoes is the making of wood and paper boxes. In the manufacture of the latter, machinery has largely taken the place of the former hand processes. The improvement in the style and appearance of the shoes in the last fifty years is no more marked than the changes in the manner of sending out the goods to market. It was a long step from the bags and barrels formerly in use, and the neat, and often highly orna-mented, individual carton in which the shoes are now packed.

The factories of the Thomson-Houston Electric Co., on Western Avenue are among the most extensive works of the kind in the country, and give employ-ment to a large number of men. They manufacture supplies and machinery for the electric-lighting companies, and their products find a ready market.

The general business of Lynn, aside from the special lines of manufacture already described, is composed chiefly of local retail trade. The section of Union street above Central square, and of Market street between Andrew and Essex streets, are chiefly given over to this branch of business. Lynn has a number of large firms engaged in the dry goods, clothing and house furnishing business, and the business in these lines is constantly increasing, the people being able to purchase about as advantageously here as in the large market of Boston. As in most manufacturing towns where wages are paid weekly, the rush of business comes on Saturday, and no more animated spectacle can be seen in any city than is presented on Market and Union streets on any pleasant Saturday evening.

Taking all things into consideration, the facilities for carrying on the leading industries, the nearness of the city to the great business centres of New England and the ease of railroad communication therewith, the excellence of her home markets, and her beautiful and healthful location, the advantages of Lynn, either for business or residence, are surpassed by no New England city.

SLIDING ROCK, LYNN BEACH.

Among the Churches.

THE first church in Lynn was formed in May, 1632, three years after the
settlement of the town. In the order of church organizations in the Massachusetts colony, this was fifth — the church in Salem first; next, that in
Charlestown, which was afterwards removed to Boston; next, that in Dor-
chester; next, in Roxbury; next, in Lynn. All the churches organized prior
to that in Lynn have ceased to be numbered among the churches of the Puritan
faith; and the same is true of those planted before it in the Plymouth colony.
Thus it may be said that the First Church in Lynn has been longer on the ground
where it was originally planted than any Congregational Church in America,
and the claim is made that it is the oldest living Congregational Church in the
world. The little house on Shepard street, which for fifty years served the pur-

THE ORIGINAL FIRST CHURCH.

poses of a church, was a very modest structure,
and the room where the people met for worship has been aptly described as "a basement
with no up-stairs," the floor being several feet
below the ground outside. In 1682 the main
portion of the house was moved to the Common, and was metamorphosed into that singular architectural curiosity known as the Old
Tunnel. The porch of the Shepard street
house finally found its way to Harbor street, where it still does humble duty as
part of a dwelling. The country was sparsely settled, and though the church
was made up of people from Lynn, Lynnfield and Saugus, the little house was
ample for all requirements for half a century. The Old Tunnel meeting-house
stood in the middle of the Common, and was the center of spiritual influences

for the community for many years. Nearly square in form, with windows somewhat irregularly placed, and the bell-tower on the center of the roof, it at a distance must have borne a striking likeness to that useful article whose name it subsequently bore. It was originally built without pews, and permission to build them was granted from time to time by vote of the town. Each person built his pew according to a plan of his own, so at last the interior of the church must have had a sort of crazy-quilt appearance. This house kept its place till 1827, when it was removed to the corner of Commercial and South Common

" THE OLD TUNNEL."

streets, and remodeled. Here it served the purposes of the society ten years more, when its new church on the corner of Vine and South Common streets was completed. This was a commodious edifice, although it might not be set down as a triumph in church architecture. On the afternoon of Christmas, 1870, the house took fire from some defect in the heating apparatus, and was consumed. The society immediately set about the task of rebuilding. The corner-stone of the present beautiful structure was laid on the 10th of the following May, and the house was dedicated on the 29th of August, 1872, with appropriate services. It is interesting to note the steps in the evolution of

SECOND UNIVERSALIST CHURCH, FORMERLY THE "OLD TUNNEL."

the present house.   Each of the five successive structures is a suggestion of the attainment and prog-ress of the people, both in material resources and in some of their religious ideas.   The first, plain and bare, without stove or comfortable seats, was not more indicative of the straitened circumstances of the set- tlers, than of the ex-reme revolt of the Puritans from the showy, ceremonial worship of the Anglican church. The Old Tunnel shows something of the returning swing of the pend- ulum, and in its day was considered

THE "FIRST CHURCH," BURNED IN 1870.

quite remarkable as an architectural achievement, and an ornament to the town. In its later years, however, the people became more fastidious in their tastes, and discovered that their historic meeting-house was becoming old-fashioned; soon the name by which it has passed into history was applied in ridicule, and

FIRST CONGREGATIONAL CHURCH, SOUTH COMMON ST.

its fate was sealed. Each of the succeeding houses shows progress in the like direction, and was the best the means of the society and the skill of the times could produce. At the beginning, when the membership of the church comprised every family in town, substantially, scattered over the territory of Saugus,

Lynnfield, Lynn, Nahant and Swampscott, two pastors were required, who, in comparison with the slender means of the settlers, were given a generous support, though Mather remarks: " The ungrateful inhabitants of Lynn one year passed a vote that they could not allow their ministers above thirty pounds apiece that year for their salary, and behold, God, who will not be mocked, immediately caused the town to lose more than three hundred pounds in the single article of their cattle, by one disaster." They were not always so poorly paid, for Mr. Whiting left an estate as good as six thousand dollars, and had, moreover, educated three sons at Harvard. In course of time Mr. Cobbet was translated to Ipswich and Mr. Whiting to heaven, and Rev. Jeremiah Shepherd was called to the pastorate, which office he filled acceptably for many years. It was under his administration that the Old Tunnel was erected, and it did service one hundred and forty-five years. Shortly before his death Rev. Nathaniel Henchman was installed as colleague, and after the death of the aged pastor, continued as sole incumbent of the pastoral office. His pastorate was filled with bitterness and dissatisfaction. He died in 1762. Following him in the pastoral office were Rev. John Treadwell, 1763, Rev. Obadiah Parsons, 1784, Rev. Thomas C. Thacher, 1794, Rev. Isaac Hurd, 1813, Rev. Otis Rockwood, 1818, Rev. David Peabody, 1832, Rev. Parsons Cooke, 1836, Rev. James M. Whiton, 1865, Rev. Stephen R. Dennen, 1872, Rev. Walter Barton, 1876, Rev. F. J. Mundy, 1885. At the close of Mr. Shepherd's ministry the church was united and prosperous. From that time until the time of Mr. Rockwood the ancient society had its ups and downs, mostly the latter, and during the pastorate of Mr. Parsons the church was reduced to five male and twenty-one female members, caused by one hundred and eight members of the church, including both deacons, withdrawing and uniting, with others, to form the First Methodist Church. Under Mr. Rockwood's earnest ministry the tide was turned. Numerous additions were made to the church, and its position in the community made much more creditable. In Rev.

REV. PARSONS COOKE.

Parsons Cooke the society and the faith had a strong and earnest champion. He impressed his vigorous personality not only upon the church, but upon the town, and under his leadership the church was placed in good financial condition and its constituency still further enlarged. The Washingtonian temperance movement, the incident of the Comeouters, and the discussions pro and con concerning Methodism, took place during his ministry, and in each of them he bore a memorable part. Like all strong men, he had many devoted friends and bitter enemies who sought in every way to undermine his influence. He wielded a prolific pen, and aside from its controversial spirit, his history of religious movements in Lynn is both complete and interesting.

The First Church hive has swarmed six times. First came out the West End or Saugus Church; afterward the church in Lynnfield; then came the secession of the majority of the church to the Methodists; afterward the church in Swampscott was set off from its membership; and later still, both the Central and North Churches. And aside from this enumeration, as many more have gone singly from its communion to other societies in the place. Despite its years, the Society is still as full of vigor and life as any of its children. A complete history of this church would be a history of the town. In the early years the church organization was substantially the municipal body. During the Quaker discussions, the church was the principal opposing factor. In the days of the Revolution the pastor of the church headed the committee of public safety, and in all the lapse of years no influence has been more potent in shaping the course of events than the old First Church.

The Central Congregational Church was organized in 1850, chiefly from the membership of the First Church, and their first church building was dedicated in December of the same year. This building was enlarged and beautified in 1864, and the following year was burned. The present handsome structure was completed in 1868, and is one of the most convenient

CENTRAL CONGREGATIONAL CHURCH, SILSBEE ST.

churches in the city. It is situated on the corner of Silsbee and Mt. Vernon streets, very convenient and accessible, though the rumble of passing trains is sometimes painfully apparent.

The North Church was formed in 1870, largely from the membership of the First Church, and though youngest among the Congregational churches of the city, is largest in point of membership; and as the section of the city in which it is located is growing more rapidly than any other, it is destined to continue to fill an important place among the churches of Lynn. The pastor, Rev. James L. Hill, has been with the church since 1875, and is the oldest in office of any

NORTH CHURCH, LAIGHTON ST.

pastor among the Protestant churches in the city. Mr. Hill was born in a home missionary cabin in Iowa, and graduated from Iowa College in 1871, and in 1875 from Andover Theological Seminary. He immediately assumed the pastorate of this church, to which he had been previously unanimously called. Under his wise leadership the church has had a steady growth. In 1878 he was chosen by the Legislature to preach the election sermon, which was done at the Old South Meeting-House. In 1881 Mr. Hill visited Europe, and in 1883 was chosen to deliver the Alumni oration at his Alma Mater. He was active in promoting the formation of the Associated Charities. As a public speaker, Mr. Hill has few superiors. His relations with his people are of the most cordial nature, and he has declined flattering calls from other places to remain here, it being, as is frequently said, a love-match between him and his people.

The second meeting-house in Lynn was erected in 1678 for the use of the Society of Friends, and was situated on a spot known as Wolf Hill, on Broad street. It stood in front of the present Friends' burying-ground, where it remained until 1723. The next house was built near the front line of that enclosure. This structure was used until 1816, when it was sold, and a more commodious meeting-house built near the same place, where it remained until 1852, when it was removed to its present

REV. JAMES L. HILL.

location on Silsbee street. The old house passed through various hands, and now serves as an office for the lumber firm of S. N. Breed & Co., on the corner of Beach and Broad streets. Now this location is being improved by the erection of a more commodious structure, and the little historic church will doubtless disappear, though its timbers are as sound as the theology formerly expounded in it. The society at present, though not large as compared with many others, is active and flourishing and, after the custom of the sect, has several ministers, Micajah M. Binford, William O. Newhall and Abigail C. Beede. Recent repairs have much improved the appearance of the church, and in its setting of trees, has a quiet, retired settled look quite appropriate to the oldest church building in use as a church in the city.

THE "OLD BOWERY."

Methodism took early root in Lynn. The Rev. Jesse Lee had introduced this religious system into Connecticut in 1790, establishing a number of classes in the vicinity of Bridgeport. The following year he came to Boston, where for a time he labored, with poor success. Shortly after he came to Lynn, on invitation of Mr. Benjamin Johnson, one of the foremost men of the town. The time was propitious in a marked degree. The dissentions which had crept into the First Church —which, with the Friends' Society, had held the field until that time—caused the many who were dissatisfied with the existing state of things to eagerly welcome any movement which offered them release. Mr. Lee came directly to Mr. Johnson's house, which stood on Market street, on the present site of Exchange building, and there the first Methodist meetings were held, whence the house came to be called the "birthplace of Methodism." Mr. Lee's coming was in February. His first class consisted of eight persons, though hundreds flocked to hear his preaching. A week after, twenty-one were added. In May the number was fifty-one. At that time the class received the sudden addition of one hundred and eight persons, who " signed off" from the First Parish. Soon the large dwelling-house of Mr. Johnson became insufficient for the worshippers, and they made his barn their sanctuary. The society became prosperous in the highest degree. Soon the society outgrew the barn, and it

THE FIRST M. E. CHURCH.

was resolved to build a church. The first Methodist meeting-house was built on the site of Lee Hall, and so great was the zeal of the builders that the house was finished so as to be used for worship in twelve days from the commencement of cutting the trees in the forest, but remained innocent of laths and plaster for a long time. This little house had no front entrance, but was approached by a door on each side, and it stood so that its front projected about eight feet into the street, as the lines now run. It served the purposes of the society until 1812, when the Old Bowery was built, and the little church was removed to West Lynn, where it afterward became the cradle of a Baptist church, and later still passed into the hands of the Catholics. The new church, with numerous additions and alterations, held its place until the present beautiful edifice was completed in 1879. This building is one hundred and twenty-three

feet in length and seventy-three in width, with a chapel adjoining, ninety-one feet in length by seventy-three feet in width. The affairs of the parish have always been ably administered, and it is now one of the most prosperous societies in Lynn. Rev. J. D. Pickles is pastor.

St. Paul's Methodist Church, organized in 1811, was the second Methodist Church in Lynn, and was the first Methodist Church in Massachusetts that was built with a steeple. The comfort of worship for many years varied according to the weather, as no stove was introduced until 1831. In November, 1859, the house was destroyed by fire, but within nine months the house now standing had been finished ready for occupancy. Rev. W. R. Clarke is pastor. The South Street M. E. Church was organized in 1830, and the house now standing was erected the same year. It was originally a

ST. PAUL'S METHODIST CHURCH.   plain, substantial edifice without a

steeple. The building has been altered and beautified until it is one of the prettiest churches in the city. The pastor is Rev. Samuel Jackson. The Boston Street M. E. Church was organized in 1853, and the church was erected in 1853. The building has been enlarged from time to time, and the church is one of the most active and efficient in the city. Rev. A. McKeown is pastor. The Maple St. M. E. Society was organized in 1851, though religious services had been held in that vicinity for many years. Their church on the corner of Chestnut and Maple streets was dedicated in 1872, and is a very neat and convenient edifice. Rev. W. B. Toulmin is pastor. The African Methodist Episcopal Society, organized in 1856, has a very comfortable, though plain, house of worship on Mailey street. Trinity Church, on Tower Hill, is the youngest of the Methodist churches in Lynn, having been formed in 1873 as a mission enterprise. Rev. Alonzo Sanderson was appointed pastor, and still remains with the society. The church edifice on the corner of Boston and Ashland streets was dedicated in 1874. The Methodist Church, both in number of societies and in membership, outnumbers any other denomination in Lynn.

The First Baptist Society was organized in 1815, but the Baptist belief found lodgment in Lynn very soon after the settlement of the town, not, however, without encountering decided opposition. As early as 1630 we find Joseph Rednap being brought to book because he could not accept the doctrine of infant baptism, and for the same reason Lady Deborah Moody, a most estimable lady, who owned a fine farm in Swampscott, was so beset by the elders of the church that she sold her property and removed to New York, where old Governor Stuyvesant received her hospitably. In 1651 three men, whose names were John Clarke,

SOUTH STREET METHODIST CHURCH.

John Crandall and Obadiah Holmes, came hither from Newport, R. I., in which state a degree of religious liberty, not dreamed of in Massachusetts, was enjoyed. They went to the house of William Witter in Swampscott, where Mr. Clarke preached, and rebaptized Mr. Witter. This being reported to the authorities, two constables went down to Swampscott and arrested them. That night they were kept under guard at the Old Anchor Tavern, and the next day were sent to Boston and imprisoned. Ten day, afterward they were brought before the courts and Mr. Holmes was fined thirty pounds, Mr. Clarke twenty, and Mr. Crandall five. The fines of the two latter were paid, but Mr. Holmes refused to pay his or allow it to be paid, and was retained in prison until September, when he was publicly whipped, receiving thirty stripes on the bare back. The whip was made of three cords with knotted ends, and the record has it that the executioner spat three times on his own hands, that he might honor justice. And in a

BOSTON STREET METHODIST CHURCH. manuscript left by Governor Joseph Jenks, it is written that " Mr. Holmes was whipped 30 stripes, and in such an unmerciful manner that for many days, if not some weeks, he could not take rest but as he lay upon his knees and elbows, not being able to suffer any part of his body to touch the bed." When he was released, two spectators, John Shaw and John Hasel, went up and took hold of his hand to sympathize with him, for which they were fined forty shillings each. William Witter was made of different metal. He was presented at Salem Court for his connection with the affair, and the following record was made: "William Witter, now comeing in, answered humbly, and confessed his Ignorance, and his willingness to see Light, and (upon Mr. Norris, our Elder, his speech) seemed to be staggered Inasmuch as he came in court meltinglie, sentence—Have called our ordenance of God, a badge of the Whore—on some Lecture day, the next 5th day, being a public fast, To acknowledge his falt, and to ask Mr. Cobbett forgiveness, in saying he spok against his conscience. And enjoined to be heare next court att Salem." After this, the coming of the Quakers and the antics of the witches kept the authorities too busy to attend to minor matters of belief.

In May, 1815, the First Baptist Society purchased the meeting-house which the Methodist society had vacated, and as if to emphasize the change of sentiment that had taken place, this house was placed on land purchased of the First Congregational Church, in full sight of their own house of worship—the very church which had persecuted the Baptists, and delivered them over to the authorities to be punished, one hundred and sixty-four years before. This building had a checkered career, being last of all occupied by the Catholics, and was

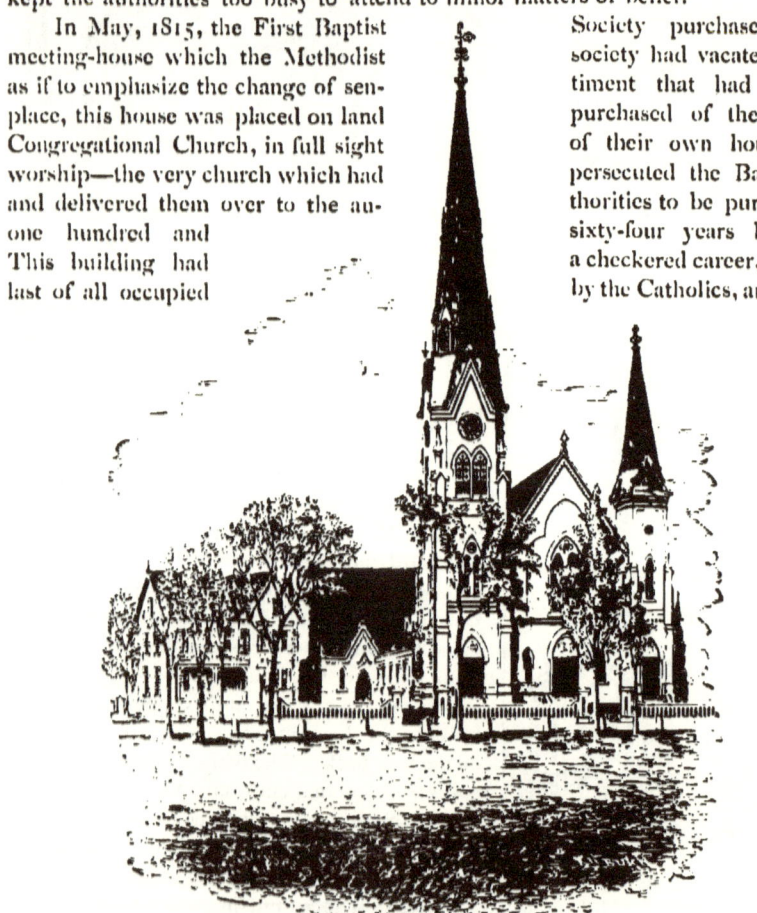

FIRST BAPTIST CHURCH.

burned in 1859. The edifice at present occupied by the society was erected in 1867. It is a commodious and comfortable house. Rev. F. T. Hazlewood is pastor.

The Second or Washington Street Baptist Society was established in 1851. Services were first held in Union Hall on Union street, and in 1858 the church on High street was dedicated. In 1871 the beautiful church on the corner of Essex and Washington streets was built, which is one of the finest church edifices in town. The pastor is Rev. Benjamin A. Greene. The Third Baptist Society, in Wyoma, was organized in 1858, and services were regularly maintained until 1876. Since then

WASHINGTON ST. BAPTIST CHURCH.

the church has been served by supplies. The East or Fourth Baptist Society was organized April 21, 1874, largely from members withdrawing from the Second Baptist Society at the time the move from High to Washington street was made. The society in the month of October following purchased the church property of the Free Baptist Society on Union street, and is now known as the East Baptist Church. The pastor is Rev. Henry Hinckley. The Union Street Freewill Baptist Church was organized Sept. 7, 1871. After the sale of its church property to the East Baptist Society, the church on High street was purchased, and now the society is in a very prosperous condition. The pastor is Rev. John Malvern.

EAST BAPTIST CHURCH, UNION ST.

The Chestnut Street Church was formed in 1857 by the Baptists, by whom worship was maintained for many years. The church building is now occupied by the Chestnut Street Congregational Society, who have within a year repaired and beautified it, and the society is enjoying a career of prosperity hitherto unknown. Rev. Jay N. Taft is pastor.

The Second Congregational Society was organized April 5, 1822, and their first house of worship was dedicated the following year. In the summer of 1852 the church edifice on South Common St. was enlarged and remodeled. This is the only Unitarian Society in Lynn. Rev. Samuel B. Stewart is pastor.

FIRST UNIVERSALIST CHURCH, NAHANT ST.

The First Universalist Society was formed in 1833, though Universalism had been preached in Lynn alternately since 1811. For three years services were held in the Town Hall, and in 1835 the society built a church on Union street, near Silsbee. In 1850 this house was enlarged and re-dedicated, and in 1864, to meet the growing demands of the society, the house was again enlarged. The corner-stone of the church on Nahant street was laid in May, 1872, and the church was dedicated Sept. 18, 1873. The tower was not completed until 1886. The cost of the church and site was $140,000. It is one of the finest church structures in New England, and an ornament to the town. This church has had a remarkable growth, and has had some very able men as pastors.

In point of membership and the number of people directly and indirectly connected with it, it is the largest Universalist church in the world, so far as is known. The Sunday school numbers upwards of seven hundred. Rev. James M. Pullman, D. D., pastor of the church, is one of the most prominent clergymen of his denomination in the country. He was born at Portland, Chautauqua Co., N. Y., August 21, 1836, and graduated from St. Lawrence Divinity School, Canton, N. Y., in 1860. During the succeeding eight years, he was pastor of the First Universalist Church, Troy, and from there he went to the Church of Our Saviour, New York city, where he remained until he was called to Lynn in 1885. During this long pastorate of seventeen years, he made a reputation, not only in the pulpit, but in all the departments of church work, which placed him in the front rank of American ministers of the Gospel. He has a marked talent for organization, and in

REV. J. M. PULLMAN, D. D.

this line he has achieved some of his most pronounced successes. During his pastorate in New York, the Church of Our Saviour was erected. He was the organizer and first president of the Young Men's Universalist Association in New York city, and has been prominently connected with the leading educational institutions of his denomination in New York. Since his residence in Lynn, his church, always a strong and active organization, has largely extended its influence, and his strong personality is felt in each line of effort put forth by the society.

The Second Universalist Church was formed in 1836, and in 1839 it purchased the church on the corner of So. Common and Commercial streets, formerly the Old Tunnel, which they still occupy. Rev. John C. McInerney is pastor.

The Christian Church was organized in 1835. The first church was built the same year on the south side of Silsbee street, next to the railroad bridge. In 1840 the present church was built, and in 1880 this was remodeled and the tower added. Rev. A. A. Williams is the pastor, having been with the society since 1877.

For two hundred years after its settlement, the Episcopal system found the New England atmosphere uncongenial. An attempt was made to form a

CHRIST CHURCH.

church here in 1819.   Services were continued in the Lynn Academy for some two
years, when they were abandoned.   In 1834
a society was formed, which took the name
of Christ Church.   Occasional services were
held during that year, and regular service
was begun on the first Sunday of January,
1835, at Liberty Hall.   These services were
continued, with little interruption, for two
years, and July 20, 1837, a church edifice
which had been erected during the year
was consecrated.   This modest structure
stood on North Common street, between
Franklin avenue and Hanover street.   Meetings were maintained until 1841.   In 1844 a
reorganization was effected.   The name now

INTERIOR OF ST. STEPHEN'S.

borne by the society adopted, and the church edifice erected in 1837 was bought.
This house served the purposes of the society until the present beautiful structure
was consecrated in 1881.   This edifice was the gift to the society of Hon. E. Redington Mudge, as a memorial of his son, Charles Redington, a lieutenant-colonel in the

Union forces, who was killed at Gettysburg, and his daughter, Fanny Olive, who died July 3, 1879. The corner-stone had been laid on the 19th of May, 1880, and in its construction and furnishing nothing was spared that could add to its beauty and completeness. The walls are constructed of reddish-brown sandstone, with facings of brick. The style of architecture gives a happy combined effect of massive solidity and graceful outline. Viewed from whatever point one may approach it, the impression received is pleasing and inspiring, and St. Stephen's Church of Lynn has come to be reckoned among the famous churches of the country. The interior is very beautiful. Our view is taken from the rear of the main audience-room, looking toward the chancel.

E. REDINGTON MUDGE.

ST. STEPHEN'S CHURCH, SO. COMMON ST.

Mr. Mudge, at whose hand the society received this costly and beautiful trust, was a son of Rev. Enoch Mudge, a native of Lynn, but for many years resident in Orrington, Maine. His business talent was of the highest order, and he used his large fortune as a trust to be administered for the benefit of his fellow-men and the city of his adoption. His mental qualities were such as to easily place him among the foremost in any company. He enjoyed the esteem and respect of his neighbors and friends in a marked degree. The building of St. Stephen's was regarded by him, and proved to be, the crowning work of his life. The work was pushed forward with his whole energy, that his wife, who was an invalid and not expected to long survive, might witness its completion. But on Saturday, October 1, just as the work was nearly done, he was taken ill, before noon had died, and his own funeral was the first service held in the nearly completed church.

REV. F. L. NORTON, D. D.

Rev. Frank Louis Norton, D. D., is the Rector of St. Stephen's Parish. Dr. Norton was born in Norwich, Conn., and received his education in the public schools, and at Trinity College, and the Berkeley Divinity School. He began his ministry as the assistant to the Rector of St. Thomas' Church, New York, and has been himself Rector of the Church of Our Saviour, Longwood, St. John's Church, Troy, and for the three years previous to his coming to Lynn was Dean of the Cathedral at Albany, N. Y. He received his degree of Doctor of Divinity in 1884. Always fond of literary pursuits, he has published the " Priest's Book" and "The Excepts of Our Lord," both of which ran through two editions. As a preacher he is earnest and scholarly, and has always drawn large congregations. Under his ministry the church is enjoying great prosperity.

The Church of the Incarnation was organized in 1885 as an offshoot from St. Stephen's Parish. For the first few months the society worshipped in Templars' Hall on Market street. On the 25th of September the corner-stone of a new church on the corner of Broad and Estes streets was laid with impressive

CHAPEL OF THE INCARNATION.

ceremonies, Bishop Paddock and other leading clergymen assisting, and on the 21st of the February following the congregation met for worship for the first time in the beautiful stone chapel. The work on the church will go forward as rapidly as possible. While the society were still worshipping as a mission, a call was extended to Rev. John L. Egbert of Vineland, N. J., and accepted by him. Though yet a comparatively young man, Mr. Egbert had achieved a reputation as an energetic and efficient worker. He is a native of Missouri, though most of his early life was spent in Kentucky. He completed his education at Kenyon College, in Ohio, and afterward studied law, being admitted to the bar in 1870; but a year later he abandoned that profession to prepare himself for the ministry, and graduated from the General Theological Seminary in New York in 1874, and was admitted to the priesthood in 1875. From the time of his graduation until October, 1876, he served as assistant minister of Christ Church Parish of Springfield, having special charge of the Church of the Good Shepherd, on the west bank of the river. From 1876 to 1881 he was Rector of St. Peter's Parish at Bainbridge, Conn., and during that time the church was enlarged and beautified and greatly strengthened in numbers. In the latter year he went to Vineland, N. J., where during the next four years he organized a strong society, and secured the building and furnishing of a beautiful stone church. He

REV. JOHN L. EGBERT.

entered upon his work in Lynn with the same consecration and energy, and the results of his labors are already apparent. The Parish of the Incarnation has an ample field in the eastern section of the city, and a future full of promise.

The first Catholic services were held in Lynn in the year 1835, and there-

ST. MARY'S CHURCH AND SCHOOL.

after at intervals, in various private houses, until 1848. In that year Rev. Charles Smith was appointed to the charge of Chelsea and Lynn, who fitted up a small school-house near the Arcade for church purposes. He was succeeded in 1851 by Rev. Patrick Strain, the present Rector of St. Mary's Church. In 1854 the little church was enlarged, but in 1859 i. was burned, and for two years the services were held in Lyceum Hall, which stood on the site of Odd Fellows' block. St. Mary's Church was built in 1861, and was at that time the finest church structure in Lynn. The society have now a large and valuable property, extending through from South Common to Tremont streets. St. Joseph's Church on Union street was begun in 1875, and has but lately been finished. It is a large and handsome gothic structure, costing upwards of $75,000. Rev. J. C. Harrington is pastor.

The following table contains the churches in Lynn in the order in which they were organized :

First Church	1632	Central Congregational Church	1850
Friends' Church	1698	Washington Street Baptist Church	1852
First M. E. Church	1791	Boston Street M. E. Church	1853
St. Paul's M. E. Church	1811	African M. E. Church	1856
First Baptist Church	1816	Third Baptist Church (Wyoma)	1858
Second Congregational (Unitarian) Church	1822	Chestnut Street Church	1868
Maple Street Methodist Society	1829	North Congregational Church	1870
South Street M. E. Church	1830	Freewill Baptist Church	1871
First Universalist Society	1833	Trinity M. E. Church	1873
St. Mary's Catholic Church	1835	East or Fourth Baptist Society	1874
Christian Church	1835	St. Joseph's Catholic Church	1875
St. Stephen's Episcopal	1836	Church of the Incarnation, Episcopal	1885
Second Universalist Church	1836		

Lynn has, accordingly, one church to each eighteen hundred inhabitants. The time has gone by when people were haled to court if they would not attend service in the church, and those who nodded a sleepy assent to sermons which they could not keep awake to hear were rudely awakened by a prod from the pole of the tithingman. Nevertheless the churches in Lynn afford ample accommodation for all who may desire to worship, and in the nine denominations represented it would seem that all shades of religious belief might find agreeable surroundings. Most of the churches are situated on the "fayre plaine" which lies in semi-circular form around the central cliff, and are for the most part convenient to the principal centres of population. Nearly all have bells, the St. Stephen's tower containing a fine chime placed there within the year, and the mellow harmony of the vesper calls are still "borne on the evening winds across the crimson twilight," even as they were carried in days gone by to the summer home of Longfellow at Nahant, calling into being the following beautiful lines :

O curfew of the setting sun ! O Bells of Lynn !
O requiem of the dying day ! O Bells of Lynn !

From the dark belfries of yon cloud-cathedral wafted,
Your sounds aerial seem to float, O Bells of Lynn !

Borne on the evening wind across the crimson twilight,
O'er land and sea they rise and fall, O Bells of Lynn !

The fisherman in his boat, far out beyond the headland,
Listens, and leisurely rows ashore, O Bells of Lynn !

Over the shining sands the wandering cattle homeward
Follow each other at your call, O Bells of Lynn !

The distant lighthouse hears, and with his flaming signal
Answers you, passing the watchword on, O Bells of Lynn !

And down the darkening coast run the tumultous surges,
And clap their hands, and shout to you, O Bells of Lynn !

Till from the shuddering sea, with your wild incantations,
Ye summon up the spectral moon, O Bells of Lynn !

And startled at the sight, like the wierd woman of Endor,
Ye cry aloud, and then are still, O Bells of Lynn !

Glimpses of the Town.

O F all the places I have seen," said a **Lynn** man, lately returning from a European trip, "there is none which is more beautifully situated or possesses more natural advantages as a place of residence than our own city." Making all allowances for the natural partiality of a person for the place of his birth, the sentiment will find a response in the heart of every one who has gained a full acquaintance with Lynn and her Surroundings.

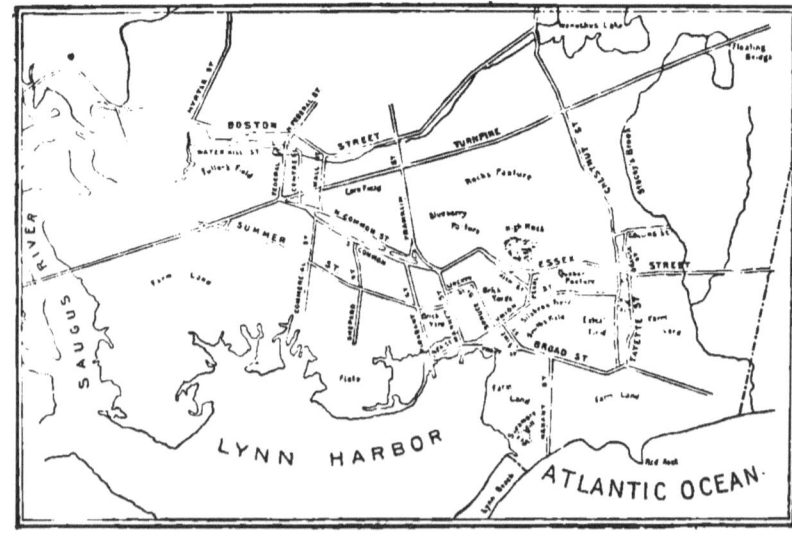

MAP OF LYNN AS IT WAS FIFTY YEARS AGO.

Thus far our attention has been devoted to historical matters and to many things relating to the business and social life of the city. As we turn now from these to obtain some glimpses of those parts of the town where our people have their homes, let us pause for a second look at the town as it was fifty years ago when there was no distinctively business section and the "shoe district" invaded almost every man's door-yard. Then every street was a residence street and many of the places now covered by busy factories or beautiful residences were cultivated as farms or still unreclaimed from the rocks and bushes. In no way can a more vivid idea of the changes wrought by fifty years be gained than by contrasting this plan of the modest town, with its less than fifty streets, with a map of the modern city with its five hundred and sixty-five streets, lanes and courts. It was along those streets that the Quakers were dragged at the cart's tail, and the witches hurried toward the keeping house until they could be transferred to the jail at Salem or Boston. It was from that town that the minute men marched to the battles of Lexington and Bunker Hill, and there Moll Pitcher practiced her magic arts. There are but few relics of those times still remaining. Many of our readers will recall the old shed, shown in the initial to this chapter, which stood on the wharf at West Lynn, when the oldest citizen now living was a boy. For many years it seemed to totter upon its aged supports, and in 1885 it finally collapsed. Waite's well on Maple street is one of the old landmarks and one can almost hear the creak of the sweep and hear the splash of the bucket, as—

WAITE'S WELL.

"Quick to the white pebbled bottom it fell;
Then soon with the emblem of truth overflowing
And dripping with coolness it rose from the well."

The old Johnson homestead, which stood on the site of City Hall, was re-

THE BLUE TAVERN.

moved to Washington street, when it found itself in the way of the march of progress, and in its new dress looks sufficiently modern; but the old "blue tavern," which stood a little farther toward Franklin street, still retains its old form in its new location on Liberty street, where it does humble duty as a tenement. It would be pleasant to go on searching out these relics of

LYNN COMMON, FROM CITY HALL TOWER.

LOOKING DOWN MARKET STREET FROM CITY HALL SQUARE.

a time gone by, but things of more living interest claim the attention.

The City Hall tower offers a fine vantage ground from which to obtain a view

THE ROLAND G. USHER HOMESTEAD, CITY HALL SQUARE.

of West Lynn and the Common, and we get a better idea of the general appearance of the western part of the city from this point than from any other. In the

SOLDIERS' MONUMENT, CITY HALL SQUARE.

early days, before the railroad and the shoe machines overturned the old ways, the vicinity of the Common was about the busiest section of the town, with the Old Tunnel Meet-

FROG POND ON THE COMMON.

ing-House in the center of the Common, and the Town House on South Common street, and banks, shoe shops and stores located here and there. The lower end of the Common, with its pleasant walks and beautiful flowers, is a very attractive spot, and the western end, with its flashing fountain, roomy stand and broad campus, offers a cool and pleasant place for band concerts, with which the city entertains the people on pleasant summer evenings, and open-air meetings, which are frequently held;

MARKET SQUARE, WEST LYNN.

and here Young America gathers as one boy on Fourth of July evening to see the fireworks.

The Soldiers' Monument in City Hall square was erected in 1873, and dedicated on the 17th of November. The design was by John A. Jackson, a native of

THE COMMON, FROM MARKET SQUARE.

Maine, but resident of Florence, Italy, and the casting was executed in Munich. The cost was $30,000. The monument is not as showy in design as are many of its class, but it is chaste and in good taste, and adapted to the place where it stands. The homestead of Roland G. Usher, which faces the monument, is one of the last remaining of the older residences which once were numerous in this locality. Its neighbors on Market street and the opposite side of the square have been swept away by the tide of improvement. At the opposite end of the Common is Market square, which received its name before Central square was dreamed of as a business centre. At one time it was the center

LOOKING UP MALL STREET.

of considerable business, which has now mostly moved down town. In 1646 the General Court voted, "on the motion of the Deputies of the towne of Linne: It is ordered that there shal be once a weeke a Market kept there on every third day of the weeke, being their lecture day." Market square was then a part of the Common, but as the lecture was held at the church on Shepard street, it is likely that the gathering of the people for trading would be near by on the Common, and possibly the modern name is a legend of the meetings of two hundred years ago. From the east end of the square we get a view up the Common which is suggested in the preceding picture. Looking at the Common from whatever standpoint, it gives the impression of roominess and invites to freedom and rest, though latterly the "please keep off the grass" sign has put in its appearance. Looking up Mall from Boston street we get a pleasant glimpse of the street

BREED'S POND.

and the fine residence of John T. Moulton on the left. This is one of the oldest streets in the town. The land in the vicinity was a part of the farm of Joseph Armitage, one of the earlier settlers of Lynn, and who led a checkered career as the landlord of the famous Anchor Tavern for many years afterward. Mall street leads us into Boston street, which is also one of the historic streets, and many pleasant residences on this old-time thoroughfare date back to the time when history verges upon romance. Back of Boston street are many pleasant short streets which run close up to the range of rocky hills which skirt the

RESIDENCE OF JUDGE NEWHALL, WALNUT STREET.

town. On the sides of these hills are many beautiful residences, and their elevated position not only places them beyond the dust and noise of the city, but affords a charming outlook over the roofs of their neighbors below. One of the most picturesque is the stone cottage of Judge James R. Newhall on Walnut street. The views from the piazzas of this charming place are among the finest in the city. Not far toward the west is Myrtle street, which merges into Dungeon avenue, leading by Breed's Pond into the woods and on to Dungeon Rock, which we visited in an earlier chapter. Breed's Pond, which, if it were not for the dam, would scarcely be a pond at all, is nevertheless one of the prettiest of the many

pretty little lakes which are so numerous
around Lynn. And our interest in it as the
source of our water sup-
ply is considerably
heightened by the score
or more of youngsters

who each summer day
resort to its shores, not
always to fish. But the water
with which it furnishes the city is
abundant and reasonably pure.

ENTRANCE TO PINE GROVE CEMETERY.

Indeed, the excellence of the water in and about Lynn early attracted the attention of
the settlers, and William Wood, author of New England's Prospect, says: "It
is farr different from the waters of England, being not so sharp, but of a fatty substance, and of a more jettie color ; it is thought there can be no better water in the
world ; yet dare I not prefer it before good beere, as some have done ; but any man
will choose it before bad beere, whey or buttermilk." He had doubtless tasted of
some of the numerous springs which
now receive the added dignity of being
called mineral springs. There are
many in our day who not only agree
with, but practice
the doctrine of the
old historian.

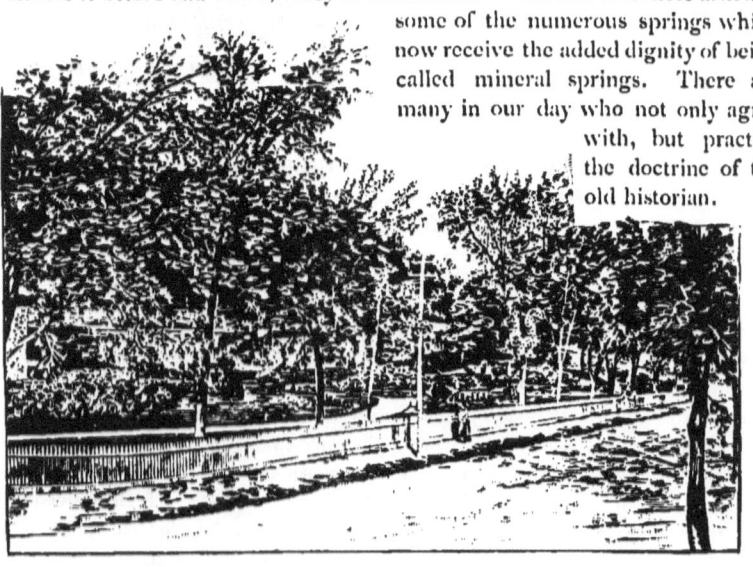

THE GARDEN IN PINE GROVE CEMETERY.

Near the north end of Grove street is Lover's Leap, a beautiful elevation one hundred and thirty-three feet in height; and half a mile west is Pine Hill, two hundred and twenty-four feet high. From the summits of these elevations a beautiful prospect opens to the view, second only to that obtained from High Rock. Returning down Washington street, we pass many pleasant residences embowered among the trees, and standing at the junction of Washington street and Western ave- nue, we look down the straight course where, in the crisp days of winter, the own- ers of fast horses try titles in friendly contests to the music of jingling bells.

LOVER'S LEAP.

Many of our younger citizens remember the time when they trooped over the Johnson pasture-fence to the circus-field in the days when Washington street existed not even in the dream of a real estate speculator. Now the view

JOHN W. HEALEY'S RESIDENCE, WASHINGTON ST.

down the street discovers a constant succession of beautiful residences, but
very few vacant lots remaining, and these may not be so long, for houses
spring up quickly in these days.

CORNER OF WESTERN AVENUE AND WASHINGTON STREET.

Highland Square is one of the pleasant places of Lynn and offers many
advantages as a place of residence, not the least among which are the good
air and the convenience to the business section of the city. Essex street, of
which the square forms a part, was for many years the thoroughfare between

VIEW DOWN WASHINGTON STREET.

Lynn and Salem, and its devious direction points backward to the time when streets
were only " roads " and were laid out for the convenience of the scattered community rather than by any system of squares and right angles. There are many pleasant residences on Highland Square, and when the city has arrived at the point

of a new High School building this locality will receive a substantial ornament. At the upper side of the square we take the steps which lead up to the pleasant stone cottage of J. W. Hutchinson, which nestles at the very base of old High Rock. Mr. Jesse Hutchinson, one of the famous family of singers, built this cottage in 1847. He was one of the pioneers into the highlands, and the pretty cottage with its picturesque surroundings, and the interesting memories of the band of sweet singers

HIGHLAND SQUARE.

Jesse, Judson, John, Asa and Abbie, who in their day sang their way into the hearts of the northern people—which cluster around it, render this to the stranger, one of the most interesting spots in Lynn. The house is now occupied by Mr. J. W. Hutchinson, the last sur-

RESIDENCE OF S. C. NEWHALL, HIGHLAND SQUARE.

viving brother of the old time favorites. While so near we can not forbear

taking one more view from the summit of the rock, breathing a thank offering, as we climb the stairs, to the Hutchinson who placed them there. The Highlands district during the last ten years has been filling up rapidly, and is becoming one of the most desirable sections of the city for residence. Hon. James N. Buffum

HUTCHINSON COTTAGE.

and Mr. Henry A. Breed were among the first to undertake the work of opening up these lands, which has been rapidly pushed during the last few years. High Rock avenue was one of the first streets opened, and soon after High Rock street and Herbert street were built. The residence of A. B. Martin on High Rock avenue and the recently completed house of Mr. Buffum on Herbert street are among the finest places in the city. Beacon Hill avenue, which strikes boldly up over the cliff next north of High Rock, is just now receiving a good deal of attention, and several fine houses have been erected near the summit during the past year. The residence of Hon. J. C. Ben-

RESIDENCE OF A. B. MARTIN.

nett, situated near the base of the cliff, has a roomy and homelike appearance and a substantial air, quite in contrast with many of the more modern designs in architec-

LOOKING SOUTH FROM A. B. MARTIN'S HOUSE.

ture. As the city continues to grow, much of the expansion must inevitably be upon the north and east sides. Already Glenmere and Wyoma have lost their former appearance of suburban villages, and become integral parts of the city.

RESIDENCE OF HON. J. N. BUFFUM, HERBERT STREET.

The eastern section of the town, while not so picturesque as that which has thus far had our attention, has the substantial and settled appearance which

RESIDENCE OF HON. J. C. BENNETT, BEACON HILL AVE.

comes with time. Nahant street, leading from Broad street to the beach was for many years the only public highway through that section. The Indian sachems, (originally pronounced " sawkum ") ruled on Sagamore hill, and what

NAHANT STREET.

on the other side of the street was not unbroken forest, was used by the settlers as farms. The march of improvement set in hereabouts scarcely a generation ago, and there are those now living who, when Ocean street was laid out, predicted that it would never be needed. How far this prediction was from the truth can best be seen by a visit to this part of the city. Almost every available

LOOKING DOWN NEWHALL STREET.

building spot has been improved, and each season sees some one or more of the older fash'oned houses replaced by a handsome modern residence. The

beautiful shade trees which adorn nearly all the streets in the older settled portions of Lynn add greatly to the attractiveness of the city. The grounds about
most of the houses in this section are spacious and tastefully laid out, and contain

LOOKING DOWN BALTIMORE STREET.

an abundance of pear and other fruit trees, to which the soil hereabouts seems
particularly well adapted. The desirability of this section as a place of residence
lies not more in the general beauty and quietness which prevail, it being quite
out of the paths of trade and travel, than in the fixed character of the population,
a large proportion of the estates being owned by the occupants. The nearness

to the beach has both its advantages
and disadvantages. The murmurings
of the waves upon the sands when old   TUDOR STREET.
ocean is in her pleasant moods, and the thunders of the billows upon the beach
when the storm king is abroad, are the every-day music—" each day hearing, yet

never learning the grand majestic anthem of the ocean"—yet the evening wind from the sea, in the hot days of summer so delightfully cool and refreshing, is sometimes laden with a chill and dampness which strikes to the marrow, unfelt in

OCEAN STREET.

those parts of the city further back from the water. Many of the best residences in this section are to be found on Ocean street. These are nearly all of modern build. And those on the easterly side have an outlook directly upon the water, and their grounds extend down to the beach. Passing down Nahant street we suddenly find ourselves upon the beach at a point where the whole expanse from Red Rock to the rocks of Nahant presents itself advantageously to the view. There is no

RESIDENCE OF EUGENE BARRY, NAHANT STREET.

more beautiful bit of water scenery upon the whole New England coast than this. Many have likened this bay, lying between Phillip's Point in Swampscott, and East

RESIDENCE OF F. W. BREED, OCEAN STREET.

Point on Nahant, to the Bay of Naples, lacking perhaps only the peculiar purplish tint so characteristic of that fair haven.   The beaches which surround this bay

RESIDENCE OF JOHN P. WOODBURY, NAHANT STREET.

have for centuries been the favorite breathing places of the dwellers hereabouts. Before the white men came the Indian youth held their sports there, and doubtless the Indian maidens and their lovers found an evening stroll upon its smooth sands as pleasant as their successors in our own time. The beach, by reason of

RESIDENCE OF J. N. SMITH, OCEAN STREET

its extent, is thought to have given the name to this region the root of the name Saugus signifying great, or extended. To the Indians the beach was a constant source of food supply, and to the early settlers a never-failing barometer. William Wood, the early writer before quoted, says of it: "Vpon the South side of the Sandy Beach the sea beateth, which is a true prognostication to presage stormes and foule weather, and the breaking up of the Frost. For when a storme hath been or is likely to be, it will roare like Thunder, being heard sixe miles; and after stormes casts up great stores of great Clammes which the Indians, taking out of their shels, carry home in baskets." The beach is now one of the most popular resorts in the vicinity, the beauty of the place and the conveniences supplied by mine host of the Hotel Nahant attracting visitors from all directions.

Out on the point of Red Rock, which juts abruptly into the waters, having Deer Cove under its lea and Humphrey's Beach stretching out toward Swampscott on the other side, we get a still better view of the bay and its setting. This has always been a favorite resting spot with the people of Lynn. In the foreground Egg Rock stands up out of the water seemingly twice its actual height. On either hand is the sandy beach, smooth and hard as a floor, with waves constantly dancing forward and backward—the same of which

Mrs. Sigourney sang, mayhap sitting on this very spot, and with her words we close this chapter of Glimpses of Lynn.

"The sand beach and the sea—
Who can divine
Their mystic intercourse, that day and night
Surceaseth not? On comes the thundering surge,
Lifting its mountain head, with menace stern
To 'whelm the unresisting; but impelled
In all the plenitude of kingly power
To change its purpose of authority,
Breaking its wand of might, doth hurry back;
And then, repenting, with new wrath return.
Yet still that single silvery line abides
Lonely, and fearless, and immutable.
God gives it strength.
So may He deign to grant
The sand-line of our virtues power to cope
With all temptation. When some secret snare
Doth weave its meshes round our trembling souls,
That in their frailty turn to Him alone,
So may He give us strength.

HOTEL NAHANT AND LYNN BEACH.

$\mathcal{O}$rganizations.

THE person who even casually studies the social developement of Lynn, though he goes no farther or deeper than the pages of the Directory, will be struck by the large number of organizations of different kinds which have not only the official paraphernalia peculiar to such, but permanent places for holding stated meetings. Not reckoning the municipal and business organizations, there are nearly one hundred and fifty societies, whose range of activities cover nearly every phase of the social life of the city.

The charitable institutions should perhaps first claim our attention. The Home for Aged Women is delightfully situated at the upper end of the common,

HATHORNE HOUSE.

on Market Square. The building, which has a decidedly classic appearance, was erected in 1832 for the Nahant Bank, which went the way of unsuccessful enterprises, four years later. It was occupied by the "Home" in 1876. This worthy charity is under the care of a board of trustees, of whom Mr. George K. Pevear is President and Hon. Wm. F. Johnson is Secretary. Mrs. Hattie E. Walsh is Matron.

Of all our public institutions perhaps the Lynn Hospital appeals most directly to the masses of our people. The hospital buildings are pleasantly situated on Boston street, near Washington, upon what was formerly known as the Hawthorne estate. Strawberry brook flows by the door, and in front rise abrupt, woody hills, with here and there a porphyry ledge breaking through the soil. The surroundings are quiet and beautiful. In early times this quarter was known as Mansfield's end. The old mansion standing at the time the Hospital corporation purchased the property was long ago known as the Deacon Farrington house, and afterward it was occupied by Capt. John White of the United States Navy, and is said to have been the house in which Lafayette was entertained when he visited Lynn. Subsequently it was occupied by Rev. Mr. Barlow, second minister of the Unitarian society, and later still by William Hawthorne, from whom it took its name. The old house now forms a part of the hospital buildings, and with the exception of new surroundings and a new coat of paint retains its original aspect. The complete

LYNN HOSPITAL.

usefulness of the Hospital is beyond expression. Aside from the case of accident which are almost daily treated, there is the unspeakable comfort of knowing that in the time of greatest need there is a place where the best of care and skill is always at command, and the poorest patient in the Hospital receives as good care and attention as the wealthiest citizen can obtain. The institution is maintained entirely from gifts, and has thus far received a generous support.

The Associated Charities was formed in 1886 for the purpose of systematizing and regulating the general charitable work of the city. Through the investigations of the Society's agents it has been possible to distinguish between the deserving poor and those who have made it their calling to impose upon the charitably inclined in the community. The Society's headquarters are at Lee Hall, where the Registrar, Miss Hannah M. Todd is in constant attendance. Cases of destitution reported here, receive prompt attention.

The Children's Home, on Tower Hill, is a two story wooden building erected in 1881, situated in one of the most sightly and beautiful spots in Lynn. The purpose of the home is to provide suitable nurture and education for ex-

CHILDREN'S HOME AND CITY ALMSHOUSE.

posed young children, to save them from the stigma of work-house life, and oftentimes from the worse influences of degraded homes. Our view takes in both the Home and the Lynn Almshouse which is situated near ot it.

The Massachusetts Society for the Promotion of Temperance and Inebriates' Home is pleasantly located at No. 19 New Ocean street, near the beach, and having an outlook over the bay. The name of the institution expresses its design, which is the care and treatment, with a view to cure, of those addicted

MASSACHUSETTS TEMPERANCE HOME.

to the drinking habit. Mr. Frank M. Flynn, who has for many years been prominent in reform temperance movements in Lynn, is superintendent.

The Grand Army of the Republic occupies a position of large influence and usefulness, having an active membership of one thousand and twenty-nine, and during the nineteen years of its existence fourteen hundred and ninety-two ex-soldiers and sailors have been connected with the organization. When it was first started it met with little favor. There were but ten charter members, and the first headquarters were in Washington Hall, now remodelled into the Boscobel Hotel. The Post was poor, and its progress during the first few years was slow. So poorly equipped was it that in the initiation of its first recruit,

GEN. LANDER POST 5 G. A. R. HEADQUARTERS.

Capt. J. G. B. Adams, they had to go to a neighboring house to borrow a bible upon which to administer the obligation; but perseverance and pluck won the day; the prejudices were overcome and the foundation laid for the wealthiest Post in the country. Post Five now owns the Coliseum on Summer street, erected in 1882, at a cost for buildings and land of $30,000, and the beautiful new building on Andrew street, erected in 1886, at a cost of $37,000. Both these valuable estates are held by the Gen. Lander Building Association, free from all incumbrance. In addition to the cost of the buildings the post has, since its organization, disbursed over $75,000 in charity.

Y. M. C. A. BUILDING.

The Coliseum is the largest public hall in Lynn, and is much in demand for political and social gatherings. The new building on Andrew street is fitted up with every convenience which can add to the comfort of the comrades. Post 5 takes its name from Brig. Gen. Frederick West Lander, a resident of Lynn, who distinguished himself in the Virginia campaign of 1861, and whose death in 1862 closed a career that gave promise of great brilliancy.

The introduction of Freemasonry into Lynn dates back nearly to the beginning of the present century. Mt. Carmel Lodge was chartered in 1805, and for many years continued an undisturbed existence. About 1827 the city was in common with many other parts of the country, stirred to its depths by the anti-masonry excitement. On the 1st of April, 1857, Mr. Jacob Allen of Braintree gave an exhibition of the alleged mysteries of that institution at Liberty Hall, on the corner of Essex and Market streets, and on the 6th the inhabitants in town meeting solemnly voted that they regarded Freemasonry "as a great

ODD FELLOWS' HALL.

moral evil," and its existence "as being dangerous to all free governments."
An anti-masonry party was formed which for several years run the politics
of the town, and a newspaper—The Lynn Record—turned its guns upon
the order. The result was that the masons kept very quiet, and several lodges
surrendered their charters. Mt. Carmel Lodge discontinued its meetings for
about twenty years, when the excitement having cooled, they were resumed.
Lynn has now three lodges, one commandery and one chapter, with a large
membership.

The Independent Order of Odd Fellows was introduced into Lynn in 1844,
near the close of the anti-
masonry excitement, the
founders claiming that it was
free from those things which
had been deemed objectionable in the more ancient society. The Bay State Lodge
was the pioneer, and has
been followed by Provi-
dence, West Lynn, Richard
W. Drown and Glenmere
Lodges, and by Beulah and
Myrtle Lodges Daughters of
Rebecca; also, Palestine and
Lynn Encampments, and
Grand Cantons Lucerne and
Palestine, Patriarchs Mili-
tant, a new military degree.
Odd Fellows' Hall on the
corner of Market and Sum-
mer streets was erected in
1871-2 by the Odd Fellows'
Hall Association. It occupies the site of the old Lyceum building, and is one of
the most ornate buildings in

RICHARD W. DROWN.

town. Richard W. Drown, for many years one of the prominent morocco
manufacturers of Lynn, was very active in promoting the principles of Odd Fel-
lowship. He was a Past Grand in Bay State Lodge, and for a long time Degree
Master of that body. He also held numerous offices in the Grand Lodge.
He was chosen Grand Master of the Grand Lodge during what proved to be his
last sickness, it being conceded by all members of that body that his services
to the order merited such recognition, and the Grand Officers came to Lynn
and to his bedside to install him. He died in 1877. Richard W. Drown Lodge
instituted in 1881, is called after his name.

The Knights of Pythias have two large lodges, both organized in 1870,
Everett Lodge and Calanthe Lodge. Their hall is in Tremont block, corner of

Tremont and Market streets. The Knights of Honor, Order of United Friends, United Order of Pilgrim Fathers, Order of United American Mechanics, American Legion of Honor, and numerous other protective and benefit associations, hold regular meetings in different places. Many of the societies are uniformed, and street parades are always in order, and the accompanying scene on Munroe street is reproduced almost any day in the summer and autumn months.

The labor organizations of Lynn are numerous and powerful, and extend to nearly every branch of industry, and all except the Lasters' Union are enrolled with the Knights of Labor. The first assembly of this organization was formed in Lynn June 22, 1878, and was known as Assembly No. 715. There were only eight or ten present at the first meeting, and the organization was kept very secret for some months. There are now thirty-four assemblies with a membership of about twelve thousand. The discipline of the organization is very strict, and they have by this means been able practically to dictate prices in many departments of labor. The Lasters' Union has held aloof from the Knights. Like the Brotherhood of Locomotive Engineers, this organization seeks not only to secure good wages for its members but to educate them in the details of their craft, so they may become good workmen. This organization originated in

A TYPICAL STREET SCENE.

Lynn in 1879, and there are now about fifty unions in the country, with a membership of some ten thousand. The Lynn Union has been very successful in the holding of fairs and other methods of raising money, and they are about to erect a hall for their use on Andrew street, near Music Hall.

The Shoe & Leather Association is an organization of the manufacturers to meet the demands of the labor unions. The result of these different organizations has been that the principle of arbitration has been adopted, and a permanent committee from each organization now meets whenever any question arises requiring settlement between employers and their workmen. Thus far the system has been found generally satisfactory.

The Young Men's Christian Association occupies the second floor of its handsome building on the corner of Market and Liberty streets. The Association does a large and good work among young men; Mr. George C. Herbert is President, and Mr. John E. Gray is General Secretary. A committee of the Association has the administering of the Tolman temperance fund. The upper stories of this building are occupied by the different Masonic bodies.

Lee Hall stands on the site of the Old Bowery church, and is the head quarters of the Park Club, one of the most prominent social organizations in the city; the Club occupies pleasant rooms on the second floor, and is frequented chiefly by our older business men.

FIRST NATIONAL BANK.

The Oxford Club has a younger and more active constituency. Their rooms in the First National Bank building, on the corner of Broad and Exchange streets, are fitted up with a view to the comfort and enjoyment of the members. The annual Charity Ball of the Club is the great social event of the year, the proceeds

HIGHLAND SCHOOL.

tem, divided among the worthy charities of the city.

In her public school system, not only in respect to the appearance and equipment of the buildings, but also the general grade of excellence in methods and attainment Lynn is second to none of our New England cities. These consist of one High School located on High street, seven Grammar and sixty-four Primary schools. The High school building is old fashioned, and while good for the time when it was erected, is scarcely up to the requirements of a modern city, and will doubtless be replaced by a more

COBBET SCHOOL, FRANKLIN ST.

suitable structure before many years. The three pictures of school houses show the different styles of architecture adopted in their construction. The Cobbet School on Franklin street is one of the finest Grammar school buildings in Essex County. A feature of our public school system is the free evening drawing school held from October till April, four nights each week. The large number who have availed themselves of its advantages have proved its popularity and usefulness. In addition to the public schools

SHEPARD SCHOOL, WARREN ST.

there are numerous schools under private auspices of considerable excellence. St. Mary's Parochial School is the largest of these, and has several hundred children under its instruction.

The Lynn Fire Department has a high reputation for efficiency and general excellence. The apparatus consists of five Steam Fire Engines of the most improved patterns, one Chemical Engine, four Hose Wagons, and two Hook and Ladder Trucks. The prin-

BROAD STREET ENGINE HOUSE.

cipal engine-house and headquarters of the department are on Broad street, near Market. This is a handsome building, affording accommodations for three engines, two hose carriages and one hook and ladder truck, offices for the Chief Engineer and assistants, and sleeping accommodations for those men, who are always on duty. In the house on Fayette street is located Steamer No. 5, and in the Federal street house Engine No. 3, Hose No. 3 and Hook and Ladder No. 2, and one hose company is stationed on Chestnut, near Pond street. The Chief Engineer of the fire department is Mr. Abram C. Moody, and much of its present state of excellence is due to his energy and faithful oversight

CHIEF ENGINEER A. C. MOODY.

and the strict discipline which he enforces. Lynn has never yet been visited by any disastrous conflagration, which is attributed in a large measure to the careful watch and prompt service of the department.

FAYETTE STREET ENGINE HOUSE.

The system of protection against fire in vogue in nearly every city and town of any considerable size throughout the country, had its birth in the brain of a Lynn inventor. Mr. Joseph Jenks was a mechanic of considerable original genius, and came to this country from England to work as founder in the Iron Works, and where he produced the first castings made in the New World. His inventions in saw-mills and scythes were among the first for which the "patronage" of the government, as patents were then termed, was sought: and in 1654 the town of Boston voted that the "Selectmen have liberty to agree with Joseph Jynks for Ingins to carry water in case of fire, if they see cause so to doe," and it is supposed that they saw "cause," for some years after, the town voted to have "the water Engine for the quenching of fire, repaired." The step from that modest little "Ingin" to the latest productions in the same line is a long one, but the principle of throwing a stream of water to the top of a burning

FEDERAL STREET ENGINE HOUSE.

building by means of a force pump has not been much improved upon—only the methods of applying it have been changed. In Lynn were several hand fire engine companies, and many of our first citizens can remember the days when they " run with the machine," and no other cup of hot coffee will ever attain to the perfection of flavor of that served by the ladies of the town, after a successful midnight battle with an incipient conflagration.   The first steam fire engine was brought to the city in 1864, and received the name of " The City of Lynn." This machine did honorable service for many years until replaced by others of more modern build.

The Lynn Public Library is one of the most useful of our public institutions. It was founded in 1862, having for a basis the collection of the Lynn Free Public Library, a corporation organized in 1855, which had in turn inherited the treasures of the First Social Library incorporated in 1819.   The collection now numbers upwards of thirty-two thousand volumes, which find scanty accommodations in the right wing of the City Hall building.   The Library is under the government of a board of trustees, of which Mr. Edward S. Davis is president. Mr. J. C. Houghton is librarian, a gentleman by taste and acquirements eminently fitted for the position.   It is hoped that the city government will take early measures to provide enlarged accommodations for the Library which is constantly growing, and extending its influence for good among the people.

The last of our public organizations of which our limits permit mention is the Lynn Free Public Forest, a voluntary association to preserve for public use some portion of the wooded section north of the city.   Several different parcels of ground in this wild and beautiful region have already been secured.   Each year the society holds a field day, when with mysterious druidical rites, the sylvan gods are honored and the lands dedicated to the use of the people forever. These ceremonies are conducted with a good deal of spirit and are always largely attended.   It is proposed that at some future time the lands thus secured shall form the nucleus of a public park, which may be made to include Dungeon Rock and the region round about.   In this event the city would not only obtain a park of rare natural beauty, but the romantic legendary and historical associations which cluster around would invest the place with a never-dying interest both to citizen and stranger.

THE OLD LYCEUM BUILDING.

Some Lynn People.

MANY of the family names of Lynn have become so interwoven with her history as to be a part of it. The names of Ingalls, Burrill, Newhall, Breed, and many more were borne by the earliest settlers, and at no time since have some of their descendents not been prominently identified with the affairs of the town. In his charming book on "Lin," and also in his Annals, Judge Newhall has done some of his most valuable work in connection with these family names; and through his efforts the youth of the future, when it shall have come to be esteemed a sufficient honor that his ancestors had a part in founding our free institutions, may climb his family tree with ease and dispatch.

The earliest settlers were generally men of quiet lives and deeply engaged in the care of their virgin acres, but in their descendents their names have become widely known. George Bancroft came to Lynn in 1630 and died in 1637, and George Bancroft the historian is his lineal descendant. The name was at that time spelled Barcroft. Edward Holyoke, who lived near Holyoke street, was one of the strongest characters in the town, and his grandson was President of Harvard College. Thomas Newhall came to Lynn in 1630, and his son Thomas, born the same year, was the first white child born in Lynn. He would seem to have become a sort of joint heir to the promise to Abraham, for although his seed are not as numerous as the stars of heaven or the sands of the sea-shore, more people in Lynn are called by his name than by any other. At one period there were eight people here by the name of James Newhall, and to distinguish them their neighbors had recourse to the nicknames, Squire Jim,

Phthisicy Jim, Silver Jim, Bully Jim, Increase Jim, President Jim, Nathan's Jim, and Doctor Jim.

John Burrill, who was grandson of the first settler of the name, was a Representative in the General Court for twenty-two years, was Speaker of the House ten years, and Councillor in 1720; and in these responsible offices he acquired a high reputation for integrity and ability. His gravestone may still be seen in the Old Burying Ground, with its long and quaint epitaph, and in his will he bequeathed forty pounds to the First Church "toward ye furnishing of ye table of the Lord. Many others of his name achieved honorable distinction in public positions, and the family came to be facetiously called the Royal Family of Lynn. Chief Justice, and afterward Senator Burrill of Rhode Island, was descended from this Lynn family.

William Gray, better known as Billy Gray, in his day the most famous and wealthy merchant in New England, was a native of Lynn, though in his later years a resident of Boston. It would be a pleasure to linger among these honored names, about which clusters so much of never-dying interest, but we must pass from them to some of the more familiar names of our own time.

ALONZO LEWIS.

Perhaps no three men have done more to perpetuate the name and fame of our city than have her three historians. Alonzo Lewis was by profession a civil engineer of wide reputation, and doubtless the familiarity with the real estate lines and titles, gained only by the patient research which his calling made necessary, led him to undertake the compilation of the history of the city. The early records of the town were in a state of almost inexplicable confusion, and very many were lost; in consequence, the labors of the historian were both perplexing and arduous. The first edition of his History of Lynn appeared in 1829 and the second in 1844. A third edition was in contemplation when he died in 1861. This work of Mr. Lewis was carefully and gracefully performed, both volumes are richly suggestive and instructive. Mr. Lewis also published a volume of poems of much merit, and wrote at times upon various topics of current interest. He was also interested in everything that pertained to the welfare of the city. He laid out the road to Nahant, suggested to the government the idea of the Egg Rock Light, and named many of the streets of the city.

Intimately connected with the name of Alonzo Lewis is that of Judge James R. Newhall. Although following the laborious profession of the law, in which he was successful, he has nevertheless found time for much literary work of a historical nature. He took up the history of Lynn where Lewis left off, and in 1865 published, under the joint names of himself and his predecessor in the work, a handsome volume in which he continues the story of

Lewis through the later years and adds largely to the record of the earlier years from the results of his own investigations. In 1880 he published a volume entitled " Lin, or the Jewels of the Third Plantation," in which in a quaint, gossipy, delightful style he treats of the prominent characters of the early settlement, together with numerous legends and traditions which cluster around the early days. In 1879 he was selected to prepare the memorial volume published in connection with the two hundred and fiftieth anniversary of the city, and in 1883 he published a volume of "Annals," in which the history of the city is brought down to that year. In early life Judge Newhall was an adept at the printer's trade, and not a little of his literary work has been done at the case, his thoughts taking form in the type, ready for the press.

JUDGE JAMES R. NEWHALL.

His racy, garrulous style lends a fascination to his books not often found in works of their class.

Mr. David N. Johnson, in his Sketches of Lynn, published in 1880, has pictured with almost photographic faithfulness to detail, many features of the business and social life of the city in the first half of the present century, and in this respect his work is a valuable supplement to the labors of his co-workers in the field of local history. Mr. Johnson has for several years been on the editorial staff of the Lynn Transcript, and is a pleasing and forcible writer both in prose and verse.

Mr. Cyrus M. Tracy has also done some good work in connection with our local history, having contributed the chapters on Amesbury, Lynn, Lynnfield, Nahant, and Saugus in the Standard History of Essex County. He is a skillful botanist, and in 1858 put forth a valuable work

DAVID N. JOHNSON.

entitled " Studies of the Essex Flora." He has also been a frequent contributor to the local newspapers, and many old citizens will remember the curious poetical controversy between him under the pseudonym of "Iota," and "The Lynn Bard," as Alonzo Lewis often styled himself.

While speaking of those of our citizens who have made their mark in literature, we should not forget William Wood, whose book "New England's Prospect," was one of the first books penned this side of the Atlantic. It was published in England in 1635, and its one hundred pages contained a very favorable description of the early settlement.

Rev. Samuel Whiting, the early pastor of the first church, published four volumes on religious subjects, which in their day attracted much attention. Rev. Thomas Cobbett, his colleague in the pastorate, wielded a prolific pen, and dealt with matters of political economy as well as religious themes. He was a man of great reputation, and his funeral was an event of the time, there being required, according to the veracious historian, for the consolation of the mourners, "one barrel of wine, £6, 8 s; two barrels of cider, 11 s; 82 lbs. sugar, £2, 1 s; half a cord of wood, 4 s; four dozen pairs of gloves 'for men and women,' £5, 4 s; and 'some spice and ginger for the cider.'" It must have been a very sad occasion.

Perhaps the most distinctively literary son of Lynn was Mr. James Berry Bensel. For many years he was a resident here, where he did much of his best work. His last published volume of poems entitled "In the King's Garden," contains the best productions of his pen. He enjoyed a wide acquaintance among literary men, and his early death cut short a career of great promise.

William H. Prescott, the eminent historian, was for some years a summer resident of Lynn, his estate being on Ocean street. Here he composed a considerable portion of "Phillip the Second," and did other writing.

Mr. Josiah F. Kimball was for many years editor of the Lynn News, and is still a frequent contributor to the weekly press of the city.

Of those who are making their mark upon the literature of the day may be mentioned Eugene Barry, whose short poems are familiar to the readers of the Boston Transcript; Thomas Ronayne, who writes for the Boston Pilot; Bessie Bland, who has produced much graceful verse which has appeared in the local press; S. W. Foss, of the Saturday Union, who has made something of a reputation by a peculiar literary device consisting of poetical lines of enormous length and an easy metrical jingle; Henrietta E. Dow, a most versatile writer of magazine articles and stories; Joseph W. Nye, who is one of the veteran poets of Lynn, and has written much for the local press; Frank R. Whitten, who is achieving a reputation in the field of literary criticism; and Howard M. Newhall, who, though yet a young man, has won a high position as a writer on economic topics, and his special boot and shoe articles have attracted wide attention both at home and abroad. The list might be much extended, but we must pass on with the simple wish that each faithful worker may receive the poet's reward:

"Thanks untraced to lips unknown
Shall greet me like the odors blown
From unseen meadows newly mown,
Or lilies floating in some pond,
Wood-fringed, the wayside gaze beyond;
The traveller owns the grateful sense
Of sweetness near, he knows not whence,
And, pausing, takes with forehead bare
The benediction of the air."

Hon. John B. Alley was born in Lynn [   ] 7, [   ]. H[ ]
wealthy and prominent member of the Society [   ] Friends. At [   ] [   ]   of
twelve he left school, and at fourteen, according to the [   ] custom   [   ]
time was apprenticed to learn the shoemaker's trade. He w [   ]d at [   ]   [   ]
steadily during the five succeeding years, and at the end of h[   ] t[   ] w[   ]
his time, He immediately engaged in business, at first at Cin[   ]a[   ]   [   ],
purchased a boat, loaded it with goods and floated down to New O[   ]   [   ]   a
trading expedition. The venture was successful, and returning to Lynn
gaged in the manufacture of shoes. In 18[   ]7 he founded the wholesale [   ]   [   ]
house of John B. Alley & Co., which has since stood in the front rank of the [   ] [   ]r
trade. Mr. Alley has also engaged in extensive enterprises outside of his [   ]   [   ]r
business and is still prominently connected with several western railroads, and
the abundant success which has crowned his efforts is the best commentary on
the ability and sound judgement which directed them.

But while giving careful thought and attention to the details of his large
business, Mr. Alley has found time to indulge a literary taste, has written extensively for several newspapers, and engaged actively in the political controversies
which led up to the war of the rebellion. He was an ardent anti-slavery man,
was prominent in the free soil party and was published throughout the South as
an objectionable abolitionist whom
all good southerners should avoid.
In 1851 he was a member of the
Governor's Council; in 1852 he
was a member of the State Senate;
in 1853 he served in the Constitu-
tional Convention; and for two
years was Chairman of the Republican State Committee. In 1858
he was elected to Congress, being
the first Lynn man who has been
accorded that distinguished honor,
and served four terms, all through
the trying and exciting years of the
war. He took an active part in the
proceedings of that body and in
several speeches advocated those
financial measures which became
the policy of the government in
dealing with the currency. He enjoyed intimate personal friendship

HON. JOHN B. ALLEY.

with the Senators from Massachusetts, Charles Sumner and Henry Wilson, as
as well as with Chief Justice Chase, and others prominent in the government,
whose names are a part of the history of those times.

Mr. John B. Tolman is one of our oldest and honored citizens. He was
born in Barre, Mass., eighty years ago, and came to Lynn in 1830 to engage
in the printing business, which he conducted successfully for many years, and in
addition to the ordinary business of a job office was successively publisher of the

Lynn Record, Sabbath School Contributor, Parsons Cooke, Essex County Washingtonian, new name, and numerous other publications.

JOHN B. TOLMAN.

The Puritan, then edited by Rev. which was the Record under a At length, failing health necessitated a change and he sold out his printing establishment and engaged in real estate transactions, and has since held many important positions in connection with private and corporate interests. The success of Mr. Tolman may be attributed to three very commonplace principles—abstention from foolish and expensive habits, unremitting industry, and strict honesty in all transactions. He has also found opportunity for extensive travel both in this and foreign countries, and has taken a notable part in the work of temperance reform. His gifts to this cause and other charities have been munificent, and by the bestowal of the Tolman Fund to the Y. M. C. A., he has secured that which many who devote a portion of their substance to the public good deny themselves, the pleasure of seeing the work which he planned in process of accomplishment.

Hon. William F. Johnson has for many years been a prominent figure in Lynn affairs. He comes of the old Quaker stock and was born and reared on the Johnson estate at Nahant, in the old mansion now standing opposite the Post Office, in which house his father, Caleb Johnson, was born and lived until he died at the advanced age of 90 years. The subject of our sketch was sixth of a good old-fashioned family of ten children. His early life, with the exception of one year spent in European travel, was devoted to farming and grocery business. At various times since 1852 he has served the city in the several capacities of assessor, alderman and mayor. His term in the latter office was in 1858, a time of great financial depres-

HON. WM. F. JOHNSON.

sion, and his administration was marked for its econ...
affairs, and its strict enforcement of the laws regul........ments. In 1862
and 1863 he represented the Essex first district in the S..... Senate...: in 1864
was commissioned as State Paymaster by Governor Andr........ to de S. Washington, to pay the State bounty to soldiers that were cred....... Mass.chusetts.
Mr. Johnson has been identified with most of the temperance movements and
charitable works of the city, and was an incorporator of the Hom. for Aged
Women and its Secretary since its organization, and an incorporator of the Lynn
Hospital and for two years its President. He was for many years connected
with St. Stephen's Episcopal Church, and is now an active member of the
Parish of the Incarnation. He is now and has been for many years engaged
in the insurance business, and in June last received his twenty-first election as
Secretary of the Lynn Mutual Fire Insurance Company.

Hon. James N. Buffum has
for nearly three score years been
in active business in Lynn. The
name is one of the oldest in the
country, the first representatives
having come to Salem from England in 1638, and the subject
of this sketch is the last remaining representative of the seventh
generation. The family early
adopted the Quaker belief, and
one Joshua Buffum suffered for
his faith, being banished by Gov.
Endicott on pain of death. He
went to England and returned
in company with Samuel Shattuck, who bore the "King's
Missive." Mr. Buffum was born
in North Berwick, Maine, where
his grandfather had gone from
Salem. At the age of seventeen
he left home. He worked six
years in Salem, three of which
he spent with the Messrs. Hook

HON. JAMES N. BUFFUM.

in building church organs; attended one term at the Friends' School in Provi-
dence, and in 1831 came to Lynn. During the first twenty years he carried on
the business of contracting builder; later he became interested in real estate
and also engaged in a general lumber business; and still later began the manufacture of packing boxes and shoe cases, in which he is still engaged. Few have
done more for the development of Lynn than Mr. Buffum. He has erected more
than four hundred buildings in the city, and in the registry of deeds at Salem are
recorded over seven hundred of his transactions in real estate in Lynn. He laid out
Ocean street, and opened up to settlement a large section of the Highlands where
his own elegant residence now is. He brought the first Steam Engine into Lynn and

set up the first wood-planing machine in Massachusetts. He was the original promoter of the Lynn Gas Light Company ; was one of the founders of the Central National Bank, and has been connected with numerous other enterprises. In 1868 he was chosen Presidential Elector ; in 1869 he was elected Mayor, and in 1872 was re-elected to the same office ; and in 1873 he was elected to the General Court. In all of these positions he served with credit both to himself and to the city.

He became an early convert to the anti-slavery doctrine, being one of the first and strongest adherents to the Garrisonian idea. He gave of his time, talents and money freely to the cause. His house was always open both for the entertainment of the leaders, and as a station of the "underground railroad." He visited England in 1845 in company with Frederick Douglas for the purpose of awakening a public sentiment in opposition to slavery there, and he spoke to large audiences in numerous places in England and Scotland. In recognition of his efforts in behalf of the slave he has not only received the attentions of the mob who stoned his house, but also distinguished honors from those high in station both at home and abroad ; and he has many interesting mementoes of those stirring and stormy times. Although in his eightieth year, Mr. Buffum is still hale and active, attending daily to the details of his large private business.

Mr. Benjamin F. Doak was for many years a leading shoe manufacturer and a public spirited citizen, and was connected with many of the principal financial institutions of the city. He was noted in life both for strict integrity and uprightness in business matters, and for timely and generous benefactions. He was a liberal supporter of the First Universalist Church, and by his will he left to be administered by the city for the benefit of the poor the sum of ten thousand dollars, which is known as the Doak Fund. The large business which he built up is still carried on under the style of John S. Bartlett & Co.

Among the many who have been prominently connected with our leading industry, but who have retired from active business are Hon. Joseph Davis, the founder and for many years the president of the Davis Shoe Company ; Mr. Stephen Oliver, Jr., who for a long number of years transacted a large business on the corner of South Common and Pleasant streets, his factory having been remodelled into the residence of Dr. McArthur ; Mr. Warren Newhall,

BENJAMIN F. DOAK.

whose factory was next to the First Church on South Common street; Mr. Lucian Newhall, formerly on South Common street and later on the corner of Exchange and Spring streets; Ex-Mayor Edward S. Davis, whose factory was near the Frog Pond, his business passing into the hands of S... I S. Ireson, who was for very many years a prominent manufacturer; Mr. Edwin H. Johnson, who in his later years was located on Munroe street; Mr. Thomas Stacey, who was the pioneer in the carpet slipper business in Lynn, and to whose business Mr. Luther S. Johnson succeeded; Mr. Benjamin Sprague, whose place of business was on South Common street; Mr. C. F. Collin, who was the successor to Micajah Pratt's business on Broad street; Mr. Harrison Newhall, for many years located on the Common, and who built the first of the brick shoe factories down town. These, and many others who are still living and active were at one time among the leading manufacturers in the city.

Among the most prominent of the shoe manufacturers of the present day may be mentioned Mr. Francis W. Breed, who is the largest manufacturer in Lynn, and in ladies and misses' shoes the largest in New England. He has three large factories—two in Lynn, and another in Rochester, N.H., with a capacity of six or seven thousand pairs of shoes per day. Mr. Breed's rise in business has been rapid but steady. Possessing the qualities of thoroughness, address and energy in a marked degree, he has achieved success in a business where competition is very close and the favors of fortune extremely few. He manufactures nearly all grades of shoes, but has made a specialty

FRANCIS W. BREED.

of popular low priced goods, and these are sent into every part of the country. Mr. Breed gives close attention to the detail of his large business, insisting upon thorough and faithful work. He is probably one of the best buyers in the market. Mr. Breed has travelled extensively and has kept himself young while carrying a weight of care and responsibility that would have broken down many. His residence on Ocean street has a beautiful outlook over the bay, and is one of the most comfortable and homelike spots on the shore.

Hon. Josiah C. Bennett came to Lynn to engage in the manufacture of shoes in 1870. His native place was Sandwich, where he was born in 1835. In 1852 he was apprenticed to learn the shoemaker's trade in Danvers, serving his full time. He remained in the shoe business until 1865, when he removed to Boston and became interested in the manufacture of shoe tips, and later engaged in the manufacture of hats. During his first two years in Lynn he was located at No. 50 Exchange street, doing business under the firm name of J. C. Bennett & Co., with Mr. George E. Barnard as partner. In 1872 they removed to their present location and the style of the firm became J. C. Bennett & Barnard. The firm has been progressive, manufacturing only the highest quality of goods, which are put up in elegant style and find their way into every part of the country. They have the happy faculty of getting along with their help, being the only firm not joining in the lockout of 1877–8. Mr. Bennett, while giving attention to the details of his large business, has found time for

HON. JOSIAH C. BENNETT.

extensive travel, and in 1885 obeyed a call from his townsmen to serve them in the upper branch of the General Court, where he made an honorable record.

While Messrs. Bennett and Breed may be regarded as fairly representative of the successful shoe manufacturers of Lynn, there are very many others who have been conspicuously successful and whose names are familiar as household words in connection with the business of the town ; and it is a noticeable fact that nearly every prominent manufacturer in the city to-day has risen from small beginnings to their present positions by their own efforts.

Hon. Amos F. Breed has for very many years been identified with our leading industry, in which he has been a conspicuous figure. He also holds a high position in financial and railroad circles, being President of the First National Bank and of the Lynn & Boston Railroad. The first is the leading institution of its class in Lynn, and the latter, largely through the efforts of Mr. Breed, has been brought to a high state of efficiency. Its line now extends from Boston to Marblehead.

Mr. John P. Woodbury has for a good many years been identified with real estate matters in Lynn. He came here in 1845 from Andover, N. H., and for some years was connected with J. Porter Woodbury in the lumber business at West Lynn. In 1854 he opened the first real estate and insurance office in Lynn, and he continued in the business until 1867, doing the largest business of any concern of the kind in the State with a single exception. In the latter year he sold out and went abroad with his family, and on his return he, with others, organized the Exchange Insurance Company, which was soon after removed to Boston. He served the company as President for a year and a half when he resigned and has since been in no active business. Among the important local enterprises with which he was connected may be named the Lynn City Improvement Company, which carried through the Central Avenue improvement, and the Market Hall Corporation, which built Music Hall, the building being

JOHN P. WOODBURY.

used as a market for some years. He is the son of Rev. John Woodbury, whose father, John Woodbury was for many years quite a noted builder in Lynn. His residence at the foot of Nahant Street, shown on page 120 is very pleasantly situated, commanding a view of the entire bay.

The legal fraternity has a goodly representation in Lynn, and members of that profession have at times filled many positions of honor. Judge James R. Newhall was Justice of the Lynn Police Court for thirteen years, and for seventeen years previous to that he was connected with the Court

HON. JOHN R. BALDWIN.

as Special Justice. Judge Rollin E. Harmon succeeded him in that office and is the present incumbent. Mr. John W. Berry, at the present time City Solicitor, has made an honorable record in his conduct of the legal business of the city.

Hon. John R. Baldwin has been called frequently to the public service, having been appointed a member of the school committee in 1879 and served till 1886, being chairman in 1881-2-3. In 1881 he was elected to the Massachusetts State Senate and served three terms, and in 1884 he was elected Mayor of Lynn, and served for the year 1885. He is a native of Lynn, received his education in the Lynn public schools and Harvard College, and has practiced law here since 1880.

HENRY F. HURLBURT, ESQ.

Henry F. Hurlburt, Esq., fills the office of District Attorney of Essex County. He was born in Boston in 1853, and received his education in the common schools and Cornell University; was admitted to the bar in 1877, and established himself in Lynn the same year. He was elected District Attorney in 1882, and by his able and impartial administration of that responsible office has won the esteem of law abiding men of all parties. His method of conducting the law business of the county has resulted in practically taking the office out of politics, and in the the November election of '86 the public showed its appreciation of his course by re-electing him with a handsome majority.

Though still a comparatively young man, Mr. Hurlburt has attained to considerable eminence in his profession, and has come to be regarded as one of the leading lawyers at the Essex bar.

The legal profession now includes some twenty-five in its local membership. There was a time, and that not so very long ago, when they were not so numerous. It was in 1808 that Benjamin Merrill hung out his modest shingle on North Common street. Scarcely however had he got his books in order when a deputation of citizens called upon him with the request that he would leave the place. They feared the presence of a lawyer in town would lead to strife and contention among the people. He took them at their word and removed to Salem, where as a Counsellor and Conveyancer he soon won a wide reputation, and in after years he reckoned some of his early visitors in Lynn as among his best and most loyal clients; and he often laughingly referred to his Lynn experience as one of the most fortunate occurences of his life, a sort of blessing in disguise, as it gave him a celebrity he otherwise might never have obtained.

Hon. George D. Hart, Mayor of the city, is one of the few young men who have been called to that office. Mr. Hart was born in Malden, but has passed most of his life in Lynn. At the age of 17 he enlisted in Co. B, 4th Mass. Heavy Artillery, serving two years in the Quartermaster's department. Since the war he has been connected with different industries in Lynn. He served in the City Council from Ward 5 in 1885, and was elected mayor on the workingmen's ticket in December of that year. Mayor Hart possesses good administrative ability and gives his constant attention to the affairs of the city.

HON. GEORGE D. HART, MAYOR.

Hon. Henry B. Lovering is the second Lynn man who has sat in the National Congress. He is a native of Portsmouth, N. H., but his parents moved to Lynn in 1846, when he was five years of age. His education was gained in the public schools, and at the age of fourteen he began to work at the shoemaker's trade, and except the time spent in the army, or the civil service of the City, State or Nation, he has been constantly engaged in some of its departments. He entered the army at the outbreak of the rebellion and served until the battle of Opequon Creek, Sept. 19, 1864, where he received four wounds and had seven bullet holes through his clothing. As a result of his wounds he suffered ampu-

HON. HENRY B. LOVERING.

tation of his left leg, which ended his military career, and returning home he went to work at his old trade, and for several years thereafter was prominently identified with the labor movements in the city, and served on the first board of arbitration that ever convened in Lynn for the settlement of labor troubles. In 1872 and 1874 he was elected to the State Legislature; in 1879 he was elected a member of the board of assessors for three years, resigning in 1880 to enter upon the duties of mayor, in which office he served two years. During his incumbency of this office he was elected to represent the Sixth District in the 48th Congress, and was re-elected to the 49th. In both he has served on the Committees on Labor and Invalid Pensions, positions for which he is particularly adapted.

Mr. Charles O. Beede is a representative man in a line of business which has during the past ten years attained much importance as collateral to our leading industry. In his early life he learned every detail of the shoemaker's art by hard work in the factory, and from 1865 to 1873 he was engaged successfully in the manufacture of shoes, when ill health compelled him to give up business for a season. In 1874 he began the manufacture and sale of shoe manufacturers' supplies, being one of the pioneers in this

CHARLES O. BEEDE.

special branch, and his factory on Union street is one of the most important concerns of its kind in New England. Mr. Beede is also largely interested in real estate. He served in the Board of Aldermen in 1881 and 1882, and headed the citizens' ticket for mayor in 1884–5.

Col. Gardiner Tufts has been more widely and generally known perhaps, from the nature of his public service during and since the late war, than any other son of Lynn. He was born in this city July 3, 1828, and is a lineal descendant of Edmund Ingalls, the first settler of Lynn ; received his education in our schools, and learned the trade of shoemaking ; subsequently that of shoe tool maker and wood turner, and he was occupied in these industries until he entered the public service nearly twenty-six years ago, in which he has since continued. In 1860 and '61 he represented Lynn in the Legislature, and in the latter year entered the postal service in Washington, where he remained until in 1862 he was appointed by Governor Andrew, Massachusetts State Agent at Washington, in which position he served until 1870, and continued as State Agent in the business of soldiers' claims until 1876. The duties of the position of State Agent during

the war were arduous and important, having oversight of sick, wounded and dead Massachusetts soldiers of the Army of the Potomac, and more especially the inmates of the hospitals of Washington ; and the agent to an extent conducted the business of the state with the general government. During the war the agency had more or less to do with more than thirty thousand sick, wounded or dead Massachusetts soldiers, received and answered fifty thousand letters, besides telegrams ; and in fulfilling these du-

COL. GARDINER TUFTS.

ties Col. Tufts had at times a paid corps of assistants sometimes numbering eighteen persons. The agent also established a bureau for the collection of soldiers pay, bounties and pensions without charge to them. More than a million dollars were thus collected, and besides he collected from the general government war claims on behalf of the state aggregating more than $1,200,000.

Col. Tufts also served on a board appointed by Secretary Stanton for the inspec-
tion of military hospitals and prisons in the Department of Washington, and
subsequently Gov. Andrew appointed him Assistant Provost Marshal with the
rank of Lieut. Col., with a staff of military officers for the purpose of recruiting
men in the rebellious states to the credit of the loyal states. He had under his
charge the District of Northeast Virginia. In 1869 Gov. Claflin appointed him
Visiting Agent of the Board of State Charities, and for Juvenile Offenders, in
which relation he continued for ten years. After the consolidation of the Board
of State Charities and the Board of Health, Col. Tufts was appointed Steward
and Treasurer of the Reformatory Prison for Women, and in December of the
same year was elected Superintendent of the State Primary School at Monson,
which position he held five years, when he resigned to accept the superinten-
dency of the new Massachusetts Reformatory at Concord, which position he now
holds. He has been a state delegate to the Prison Congress and Conference of
Charities held in Cincinnati, New York, Cleveland, Madison and Detroit, and a
paper upon the Massachusetts Visiting Agency and Juvenile Offender System,
read by him at Cleveland, was brought to the attention of the Howard Association
in London, was there favorably received and led to the adoption of some Massachusetts features in England and her provinces. In the political and municipal
affairs of Lynn Col. Tufts has borne his part, having been Inspector, Clerk, and
Warden of Ward 6, and at different times member of the Common Council and

Board of Aldermen; and was for
several years Chairman of the Republican City Committee. It is
not often that a man is permitted to
serve the public in such important
relations for so long a time, but in
all these positions Col. Tufts has
acquitted himself with credit both
to himself and to his native town.

General B. F. Peach is a native of Marblehead, where he passed
his early life. From 1856 till 1878,
excepting the time he served in the
army, he was connected with the
shoe manufacturing firm of W. T.
Haskell in the successive capacities
of journeyman, foreman, and partner. He manifested in early youth
an ardent fondness for military affairs, and at the breaking out of the

GEN. B. F. PEACH.

war of the rebellion was First Sergeant of the Marblehead Light Infantry,
and served with that company in the famous Eighth Regiment during the three
months campaign. He was promoted First Lieut. of the same company March
1862, and was appointed Adjutant of the Eighth Regiment in August of the
same year. He was with the regiment during its nine months service in the
Department of North Carolina and in the Army of the Potomac. He was com-

missioned Colonel of the same regiment in July, 1864, being then but twenty-five years of age, and was discharged at the expiration of his term of service in November, 1864. He continued in command of the regiment as a portion of the volunteer militia of the state until February, 1882, a period of more than seventeen years, when he was promoted Brigadier General of the Second Brigade, and is at this time next commanding officer in rank to the Governor and Commander in Chief, enjoying the confidence and respect of the officers and men of his command as well as the people of the state at large.

In 1866 Gen. Peach removed to Lynn from Marblehead, and in 1879 he was elected City Treasurer and Collector of Taxes, in which position he remained until 1885, when he resigned to take the position of U. S. Pension Agent at Boston, tendered him by President Cleveland.

Hon. Frank D. Allen, though yet a comparatively young man, has attained to considerable prominence both in his profession of the law and in political life. He is a native of Worcester, born in 1850, graduated from Yale College in 1873 and was admitted to the Suffolk bar in 1876. He has resided in Lynn since his marriage to Miss Lucy R., daughter of Trevett Rhodes, in 1877. In 1880 and 1881 he represented Ward 5 in the General Court, and in 1885 he was elected to represent the fifth councillor district in the Governor's Council, where he serves upon the Committees on Railroads and Hoosac Tunnel, Charitable Institutions, Prisons and Warrants.

HON. FRANK D. ALLEN.

He has also, for two years, served on the Republican State Central Committee. While giving some attention to politics he has attained success in his profession, and as counsel for the Lancaster Bank he unravelled the tangled affairs of that institution, recovered the stolen securities and secured the indictment of the principle conspirators.

Capt. John G. B. Adams was born in Groveland, Mass., Oct. 6. 1841. and passed his boyhood and youth in that locality, and in the early summer of 1861 enlisted in Maj. Ben : Perley Poore's Rifle Battalion which later became the nucleus of the 19th Mass. Regiment. He served through the war, rising rapidly to the rank of Captain. He participated in every march, and was engaged in every battle of the Army of the Potomac in which his regiment took part. At Fredericksburg he saved the colors of his regiment from capture after eight color

CAPT. JOHN G. B. ADAMS.

bearers had been killed. He was twice severely wounded in the second day's fight of Gettysburg, and while in the advanced lines before Petersburg on the 22d of June, 1864, he was captured with his regiment, and for nine months suffered the miseries of a southern prison pen. After the war he was for some years foreman in the factory of B. F. Doak & Co., but on account of failing health he resigned that position to enter the Inspector's office in the Boston Custom House. He remained there some fifteen months, when he was appointed Postmaster at Lynn, which office he held eight years. On the establishment of the Reformatory Prison at Concord he was appointed Deputy Warden, and at the last session of the General Court he was appointed to the office of Sergeant at Arms, which important position he now most acceptably fills. Capt. Adams was the first recruit mustered into Post 5, G. A. R. He was three times chosen commander, and was for one year Department Commander of Massachusetts. He has been for eight years president of the association of Survivors of Rebel Prisons, and is chairman of the Board of Trustees of the Soldiers' Home. He has also been connected with numerous local enterprises, having been one of the incorporators of the Lynn Hospital, Lynn Electric Co., and also of the Thomson-Houston Electric Light Co.

Mr. William A. Clark, Jr., was born in Newark, N. J., June 9, 1852. He served an apprenticeship in the jewelry business, and came to Lynn in 1873. Three years later he engaged in the jewelry business which he continued successfully until 1886. In 1880 he was elected a member of the School Board, and took a prominent part in re-establishing the evening schools. In 1885 he was elected a member of the General Court and served on the Railroad Committe of which he was clerk, and was re-elected to the

W. A. CLARK, JR.

legislature of 1887. Mr. Clark was a faithful worker   efficient member. He has lately disposed of his business in Lynn and engaged in some public enterprises of considerable importance.

David Walker was born in the village of Troynholm, Scotland, Aug. 3, 1841, and came to this country when ten years of age. In the winter of 1856 he came to Lynn to engage in the leading industry of the place. During the war he served as private in the 53d Regiment Massachusetts Volunteers and the 4th Massachusetts Heavy Artillery. He was a charter member of Post 5, G. A. R., and has been prominent and active in the general work of the order. Mr. Walker has also been an efficient member of the order of Odd Fellows, being a Past Grand of West Lynn Lodge. In 1885 he was elected to the General Court from Ward 6, serving on the Committee on Labor, and his work in that body has been endorsed by a

DAVID WALKER.

re-election to the legislature of 1887. In every position to which he has been called Mr. Walker has brought the qualities of steady faithfulness and uprightness.

HON. FRANK W. JONES.

Hon. Frank W. Jones is a native of Stoughton, Mass., born in 1855, and was educated in the public schools of the town. He came to Lynn in 1872, and has followed the trade of shoemaking. He was elected as Representative to the General Court in 1884, and in 1885 was chosen to the Senate, being next to the youngest member of that body. He rendered efficient service, being especially prominent in advocating the abolition of the Contract Convict Labor System. Mr. Jones has been an active member of the labor organizations of the city, and his efforts in legislative matters have been to better the condition of his fellow workmen so far as this can be done by legislative enactment. He was also re-elected to the Senate of 1887.

Horace A. Roberts was born in Sandwich, N. II., Aug. 15, 1853, but has been a resident of Lynn most of his life. He was educated in the public schools, and after leaving school, worked for several years in the shoe business and the ice business with his father, and in 1881 became a member of the firm of B. F. Roberts & Son. He has given much of his time to temperance work, attained the high degree of Grand Worthy Patriarch in the Sons of Temperance. He was but 26 years of age at the time and was the youngest man ever chosen to that office. He has also been prominent in the Independent Order of Odd Fellows. He was chosen to represent the Tenth Essex District in the General Court in 1885, serving with

HORACE A. ROBERTS.   much credit on the Committee on Public Charitable Institutions. He was re-elected in 1886.

We are now at the end of our sight seeing in Lynn, having traced the progress of the city from the early settlement in the Saugus forest to the modern, thriving busy city, walked up and down her streets, viewed her natural and artificial beauties and attractions, examined into the public and charitable institutions, visited her churches, and been introduced to some of her leading citizens representing nearly every walk of life. In our excursion, as was inevitable from the nature of it, very many things which it would have been both a pleasure and a profit to have seen have been passed by, but it is hoped that the casual acquaintance thus gained may prove pleasant and lead to a closer knowledge and broader appreciation of our goodly city. Thanks are due the reader for his kind and genial companionship thus far, and before the final parting we would invite him to a flying trip to the Surroundings of Lynn.

Lynn & Surroundings.

CONSCIOUS of her age and dignity, Lynn sits proudly in her beautiful home by the sparkling bay, a mature and stately matron, with her five grown up daughters happily settled around her. Reading, settled by Lynn people in 1639, is the eldest of the family. Her original territory was four miles square, beautifully situated and possessing many natural advantages, but the inhabitants early lost the home feeling, and set up an establishment of their own.

Lynnfield, for many years called " Lynn End," is the second child. The inhabitants of Lynn with their original 8680 acres, feeling somewhat crowded, were granted " six miles into the country," and an inland plantation was forthwith begun. This occurred soon after the settlement of the town. The Second Parish was set off in 1712, and the town was incorporated one hundred and two years after. A summer drive to Lynnfield takes one out through pleasant suburban Wyoma, along by numerous pleasant ponds and deep ravines on this side and on that, and shadowy woods, sweet with the smell of pine and juniper. Lynnfield Village is a pleasant place, with a good hotel, a few small manufactures, stores and other paraphernalia of a well-to-do country place. The farms which lie about the village are fertile and well tilled. A branch of the Boston and Maine Railroad gives quick communication with the busy world, and taken all in all this second of Lynn's daughters is well and comfortably settled in life.

Saugus, called by the maiden name of the parent town, was set off as the Third Parish, and attained to the dignity of a meeting house of her own in 1736, but remained under the maternal wing until 1815, when she was incorporated

FRANKLIN SQUARE, EAST SAUGUS.

as a town. The Saugus river—the Indian Abousett—and the marsh—the Rumney marsh of the early settlers—divide the town into unequal parts, in each of which are many pleasant residences and fertile and well cultivated farms, and there are also manufactures of considerable importance. There are three pleasant villages in the town—East Saugus, Saugus Center, and Cliftondale—each with its peculiar attractions, and numerous pleasant spots which are sought out by picnic parties; and the Franklin Park is a favorite place for the trials of

LOOKING DOWN LINCOLN AVENUE, EAST SAUGUS.

equine speed and mettle. There are many points of interest, among which may be named the old Iron Works, the first in the new country; Pirates' Glen, the site of the Old Anchor Tavern, for many years a chief hostelry of the whole region round about; and on Lincoln avenue was the old Ballard Tavern, also a favorite inn. The site is now occupied by the residence of W. F. Newhall, Esq., but the old building is still standing a little farther down Ballard street.

The region round about Lynn abounds in beautiful drives. Good country roads radiate from the city in all directions and in a very short time after leaving

HUNTERS' CABIN, NEAR FLAX POND.

Central square one may find himself where—

"Kind nature shuffling in her loose undress,
Lays bare her shady bosom,"

and if the tourist has been shut up for a season within city walls, he may echo the sentiment of the remaining lines of the stanza—

"I can feel
With all around me; I can hail the flowers
That sprig earth's mantle; and yon quiet bird
That rides the stream is to me as a brother.
The vulgar know not all the pockets
Where nature stows away her loveliness."

Swampscott, the fourth of Lynn's fair daughters, sits dreamily by the sea, spreading her snowy skirts out on this side and on that even down to the salty rim of the ocean. The few picturesque old fish houses along the shore and the score of dories drawn up on the sands, with here and there a siene spread out to dry, are but faint reminders of the time when this was the most important fishing town on the New England coast. Now, however, the entire shore down almost to the Marblehead line has been captured by the summer resident, and the numerous tasteful cottages and beautiful villas which crown every eligible

SWAMPSCOTT.

spot, in summer teem with gay and fashionable life, but in the winter present a
formidable array of shuttered windows, the summer birds having flown back to

LINCOLN HOUSE, SWAMPSCOTT.

their winter homes. This is true however only of that portion of the town
which lies along the shore. The inland section is very much like other towns,
and were it not for the name could hardly be distinguished from the parent city.

Nahant, the youngest of the
family, was gifted both with
beauty and wilful originality.
While her sisters seem to have
been content to settle down to
quiet lives on the shore, this one
appears to have tried to run away to
sea, but found herself held back by the
shining white maternal apron string.
The beauties both of form and situation of these twin islets has challenged the

BAILEY'S HILL, NAHANT.

admiration of all who have come to know them. The Indians gave her one of the prettiest names of their language, "Nahanteau." The legend relates that Thorwald, the sturdy Norse adventurer, the first white man who approached these shores, at once became enamored of her beauty, and striking his spear into her virgin bosom exclaimed " Here it is beautiful, and here I would like to fix my dwelling." The legend goes on to state that an Indian arrow helped him to the attainment of his desire in an unexpected and unpleasant fashion, and that his bones now mingle with her soil in some unmarked spot.

The early settlers seem to have been chiefly attacted by its economical advantages as a cow pasture, no fence being required except across the beach, until Edward Randolph became infatuated with its beauty, and undertook to wrest it from them. Then an idea of the value of the gift of the dusky Duke William suddenly dawned upon them, and they arose as one man to defend their common property. Thomas Dexter saw the possibilities of gain in the fair domain, and doubtless thought a suit of clothes a cheap enough price for it, but it proved otherwise, for instead of the Nahants he got only a troublesome and unfortunate suit at law, and the only one who seems to have profited by the trade was the wily Indian who got the new suit. In later years the beautiful peninsula was again coveted, and this time gained, and the new proprietors guard the approaches to their summer homes so closely that the public

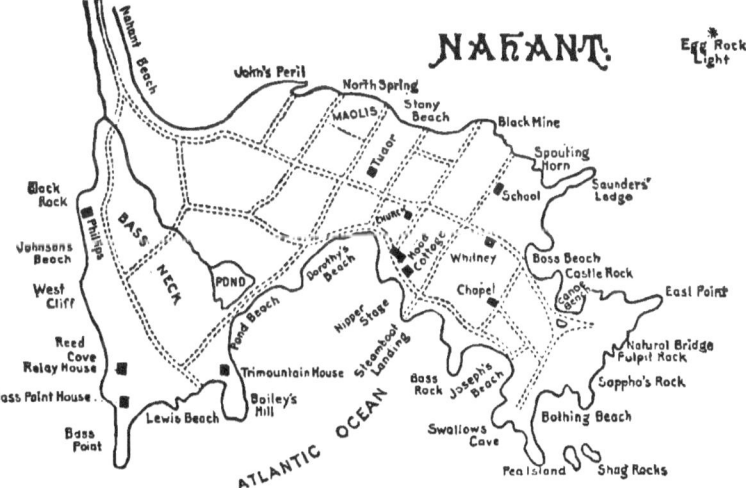

can gain a foothold only in isolated places—the Maolis Gardens on the north side and Bass Point on the south. The Nahantese cling to their acres with a grip that cash in hand has no power to unloose, and if ever Nahant becomes a popular resort the traditions of half a century will have to be reversed.

The beauties of this spot have been sung by so many gifted tongues that we need do nothing more here than to point to the accompanying chart. "If," says N. P. Willis, "you can imagine a buried Titan lying along the length of a continent, with one arm stretched out into the midst of the sea, the spot to to which I would transport you, reader mine, would be, as it were, to the palm of the giant's hand." Whittier also addressed one of his earliest poetic productions to this charming spot.

Nahant, thy beach is beautiful!—
    A dim line through the tossing waves,
Along whose verge the spectre gull
    Her thin and snowy plumage laves.—

What time the summer's greenness lingers
    Within thy sunned and sheltered nooks,
And the green vine with twining fingers
    Creeps up and down thy hanging rocks!

Around—the blue and level main—
    Above—a sunshine rich, as fell
Bright'ning of old, with golden rain,
    The isle Apollo loved so well.

            *   *   *   *   *

But fairer shores and brighter waters,
Gazed on by purer, lovelier daughters,
    Beneath the light of kindlier skies,
The wanderer to the furthest bound
Of peopled earth hath never found
    Than thine—New England's Paradise!

LYNN AND NAHANT.

Nahant has always been a favorite resort for those of refined literary tastes; there being something in its peaceful, quiet life and the character of its scenery which prompts genius to its best efforts. Longfellow constantly came hither for rest and inspiration. A part of "Hiawatha" was written here, and "The

Bells of Lynn," and " The Ladder of St. Augustine " here found their birthplace, and many others of his lyrics in which the presence of the sea is felt by the reader, were also written here under its influence.   In the Hood Cottage, Motley begun his " Dutch Republic ;" a little beyond stood the cottage where Prescott worked at " Ferdinand and Isabella," and " The Conquest of Mexico ;" on the point beyond, Agassiz produced his " Brazil ;" and Willis, Curtis, Mrs. Sigourney, and a host of lesser celebrities have sought and found its magnetic inspiration.   And one of her own sons, Henry Cabot Lodge, has well nigh overturned many of the accepted conceptions of early colonial characters by his research and keen analysis.   Longfellow and Prescott loved best the southern shore, but Agassiz chose the northern side.

The admirably kept roads lead to where the most pleasing sea views are to be had.   Notwithstanding the horse car is stopped at the town line, and the excursion steamer is warned off shore, if one can brave the jolting of a barge, or better still, command a private conveyance, the wondrous beauties of the ragged riven shores may be easily reached.   It almost takes one's breath away to watch and almost feel the mighty rush and roar of the eternal surges among the resounding sides of these cliffs and caverns.   The tawney rocks wear coats of grass-green velvet above the water line, and the nodding plumes of the sweet fern and columbine wave from the niches and hollows where they can gain a foothold.   The sea gulls sail through the air over our heads or swoop upon their prey almost at our feet, and the white sails of the numerous water-craft pass and repass before our view.   Midway between us and the Swampscott shore, rising sturdily above the waves which dash around it, stands Egg Rock, as fair in the sunlight as when the ardent youth sought to pluck from it the Floure of Souvenance for his Lady Alice who was seated, perchance, on the same promontory on which we are.   And with this quiet scene before the view we bid farewell to the friends who have accompanied us thus far in our excursions in Lynn and Surroundings.